HELLA...

the scripts

Season One

DAVE HOPKINS

&

JONATHAN SMITH

*mousehole***productions**

Copyright ©mousehole productions 2019

All rights reserved. No parts of this book may be reproduced, transmitted, downloaded, decompiled, defiled, reverse engineered, stored or eaten without the written permission of the authors.

Don't try scanning or distributing it for free either. Any attempt to do this will result in a stern look, cross words and a short fight, which we'll definitely win because we're really hard. If you're that desperate for another copy of this book, buy one, you scrounging mimsy.

ISBN: 9781679334504

www.hellanory.com

For my parents, who would have been chuffed seeing my name on a book on their coffee table.

and

for Bronagh, who likes a good scare.
D.H.

For mum, for being the perfect demon

and

for Daniel Cohen, because.
J.S.

CONTENTS

	Are you sitting uncomfortably?	7
	... Then we'll begin.	15
1	The Peculiar Case of Nathaniel Fry	27
2	Orwak Baler Is Unwell	39
3	Surplus Baggage	51
4	The Box	65
5	My Name Is Michael Crane	75
6	Char	87
7	The Movement Of Water	99
8	An Open Fire	117
9	Hellanory: Genesis	131

ARE YOU SITTING UNCOMFORTABLY?

*'After I'd finished lying on the floor,
pounding the carpet with my fists
and weeping bitter, frustrated tears,
I went off and wrote something else ...'*

Hellanory came about as a positive result of rejection.

I'd spent years – I'm embarrassed to say quite how many – writing stuff, sending it off and getting rejection slips, first by post (that goes to show how many years I'm talking about) and then, in more recent times, by email. I started long ago by writing film scripts after browsing through the Film & TV section of a bookshop in Camden Town during my lunch break and finding a book called *Writing Screenplays That Sell* by Michael Hauge. A whole world of possibilities opened up before me. Needless to say, the film scripts I wrote didn't sell and, let's be honest, probably didn't even get read. After some years of banging my head against the brick walls of the British film industry, I narrowed down my goals and aimed for television instead because, obviously, it's really easy to get into writing for television.

It isn't.

Years of frustration and a regular stream of rejection letters followed. On the whole, the rejection letters were very kind and complimentary – apart from one which simply said NO! in capital letters – and indicated that my scripts were promising, but just not *quite* what production companies were looking for. I seethed with anger and envy when I read an interview with one television writer who described how he'd got into the industry. He'd sent in a spec script, rough and structurally all over the place, but someone, somewhere had seen something in the script and had given him a chance. I burned an effigy of the writer at the stake and danced naked around the glowing embers of the pyre. Why, I kept asking myself, why wouldn't someone give *me* a chance too? After I'd finished lying on the floor, pounding the carpet with my fists and weeping bitter, frustrated tears, I went off and wrote something else and began the whole process of sending it off, waiting for a reply and getting rejected all over again.

For a while, around 1997/98, my friend Ged and I teamed up and came up with a great idea for a television sketch show, wrote a pilot script and sent it off to a few production companies. Unbelievably, on the strength of the pilot script we got an agent – a highly respected one who had his fingers in many televisual pies – and were invited in for a chat by a hip production company who told us that the script we'd written was anarchic and unique and that they'd be looking at spending £250,000 an episode on the series, possibly with a couple of big names in it to sell it to broadcasters, as we were new writers and would need some comedic weight behind us. Our eyes flicked up to the photographs of Vic Reeves and Bob Mortimer and the cream of the current comedy crop festooning the walls. We couldn't believe what we were hearing. They told us they'd be back in touch in a couple of weeks and that they'd take us out for dinner.

We left the offices in stunned silence, walked to the end of the street and collapsed in helpless laughter. We went to the pub and celebrated. We'd finally done it. Two weeks came and went. Then three. Then four. By the sixth week, when they finally called again, we were really bloody hungry and looking forward to our meal. They invited us back in to their offices and in we duly went, rubbing our hands in anticipation of a three course meal and imminent wealth.

The man who'd called the script anarchic and unique wasn't present this time round. In his place was a smug, humourless clot who shall remain nameless. He made it quite clear that the company wouldn't be taking plans for the show any further. He picked apart all the jokes in the script and kept asking us why they were funny.

We left, it has to be said, in very low spirits.

But at least we had an agent.

Well, on paper, yes. The reality was, though, that our agent wasn't really that interested in the script or sending it round to other production companies, probably because he was too busy running his own very successful one alongside being the agent for some very well-known television writers. He told us that there was no way we'd be able to sell the series as we were new writers. He asked us to submit some ideas for a forthcoming comedy sci-fi show, which we did. He told us that each idea we'd obediently submitted sounded like an episode of *Star Trek*. We asked him to give us something else to do, so he got us to send him four ideas a month for sitcoms. We felt like we were on work experience and he didn't have a clue what to do with us. I'm surprised he didn't have us cleaning the toilets. Over three or four months our attempts at sitcom ideas got ever more frantic and desperate. One attempt I came up with was set in an art gallery where the woman running it was a vampire.

Like I said - desperate.

In the end, the agent didn't even bother responding to the ideas and after a year our contract with him wasn't renewed. Quite why he ever took the two of us on in the first place was beyond me and still is. He'd given up on us before we'd even got going and, eventually, life got in the way and we did too.

*

I poked around with a few more ideas of my own, but my heart wasn't really in it any more. Things came to a head when I wrote an episode of a fake TV serial and sent it in as a writing sample to the producers of a well-known television soap. For a while – six months or so – it looked like I might be in with a chance of being accepted on the soap's writer's scheme. I figured if I got on, it would be great training and from there I'd go on to write subtle, thought-provoking dramas for the BBC. The comments I'd received about my fake soap episode were complimentary and positive to the point of convincing me that this time, *this* time, it was definitely, *definitely* going to happen.

It didn't.

At this point, I did what any sane person would do and gave up. The constant rejection was making me depressed, effecting my mental health and general outlook on life. I finally binned the huge pile of rejection slips I'd built up and stored away in a folder in the hope that one day I'd flick through them as a successful writer. Writing and dreaming up stories got cut from my list of priorities, much like an out-of-favour friend might get cut from a Christmas card list. I moved from London to Brighton, started a new job and had kids. They, quite rightly, became my priorities.

For a while, I was content but couldn't *quite* leave the writing behind. I experimented on and off with a few short films, made with a home video camera. One of the films – a fifteen second short called *No Smoking* – got shown, along with a load of others from the competition I'd entered, at a West End cinema. Sitting in the darkness waiting for my film to come on (they showed thirty and mine was about halfway through), I listened to the screams of laughter that greeted the fourteen or so before mine. When mine came on, people were still laughing at the one that preceded it but stopped when my one reached its punchline. I left the cinema furtively, keeping to the shadows.

Then I started writing children's stories. I tried to convince myself that I was doing this purely for the enjoyment of writing and my own kids' entertainment. I sent some of the stories I'd written – about two brothers called Harvey and Herbie – to a publisher of children's books. I told myself I was doing this just to see what would happen. Just out of interest. As it turned out, the publisher got back in touch and said yes, they were interested but that the stories I'd written were very short. Would I be able to expand on them a little and do something a bit longer? Yes I bloody well would, I thought, ignoring the fact that the reason the original stories worked was because they were short. I sent them a much longer story called *Dinosaur Hunt* featuring the two brothers and waited for a response. A month went past. Then another. Then another. After five months I sent a tentative email asking the publisher what they thought of the book. I got a reply telling me that yes, they liked what I'd done and would be discussing it at a forthcoming meeting which just happened to be taking place later that very week.

I received a further response quite quickly after that. It had been decided not to proceed with the book as it was generally felt that it wasn't quite what they were looking for. I deleted the email and the stories, threw my hands up in the air, headbutted a radiator, screamed with frustration and went back to being a father.

Then, some years later, I got a job as a teacher at a language school in Brighton and met Jon Smith.

Jon and I bonded over a mutual hatred of the hilariously awful text books we as teachers were forced to use in our lessons, as well as the discovery that we shared the same first memory of *Doctor Who*, specifically the moment in the first Jon Pertwee story, *Spearhead from Space*, when Auton shop dummies came to life and started blasting people to death with their wrist guns in a blaze of unconvincing 1970s TV special effects. We also shared – and continue to do so – a love of music, old science fiction films, a sense of the absurd and good TV comedy.

Jon and I left the school nearly three years later within a month of each other. I went off to, in theory, teach privately via Skype and he went off, in very real terms, to go and live in deepest, darkest, rural Norfolk and look after his elderly mother. We stayed in touch and rather shyly sent each other our past writing attempts. Jon's stuff had a mad, relentless quality that put me in mind of a demented Alan Bennett. At about the same time, I started to write again. Being a teacher and dreaming up inventive lessons had satisfied my creative side and I hadn't thought of writing anything during those three years but now that I was no longer teaching (the Skype lessons I'd advertised had no takers) the creative urge was back with a vengeance. I scoured the BBC Writersroom website and discovered that they were asking for submissions for their Drama submission window. I wrote something for it and sent it to Jon for his critical input. One thing, as they say, led to another and before we knew it we were collaborating on an idea for a whole TV series. We came up with a couple of sample episodes and a series outline and duly sent them off.

The series didn't get anywhere, but it didn't seem to matter. We'd both rediscovered the writing bug and, crucially for me, the joy of writing just for the sake of it, without fixating on someone, somewhere, making the script as the end result.

At the end of 2017, I got asked by my friend Dan Whaley to choose three songs and talk about them as a guest on his excellent show *Out Of Limits* on Burgess Hill Community Radio. Seeing him sitting behind the studio control console presenting his show and clearly loving every minute of it had a profound effect on me and I started toying with plans for doing a show of my own. It was also about this time that Jon announced, cryptically, that 2018 was going to be 'all about the podcast.' How right he was. He came up with the sensationally eclectic *No More Love And Flowers* podcast and I started writing and recording my own show, *In The Basement With The Dancing Monk*.

I loved the whole DIY approach, recording the shows using nothing more than a laptop, a microphone, a large back catalogue of 1950s rockabilly, R&B, rock and roll, 60s pop and soundtrack selections from across the eras. I went at the writing and recording of the shows like a madman, recording episodes months in advance of their broadcast dates. I'm still, as I write this, working through the backlog of recordings. Mucking about with sound effects and recording software, I started thinking of ways I could go beyond a music show, using readings of some of my own stories, set to a weird, aural background. I told Jon about this and suggested that we include some of these stories in *No More Love And Flowers*. But Jon pointed out, quite rightly, that the idea needed a whole podcast of its own to fully breathe. A separate show that would allow us to write and produce whatever we bloody pleased without having to throw ourselves at the mercy of the opinions and acceptance of other people.

What you have in the following pages are the scripts for the first series. They're pretty much identical to their recorded versions apart from a few minor tweaks and alterations that came about during the recording process. We hope you enjoy reading them as much as we enjoyed writing them.

Now.

Are you sitting uncomfortably?

Dave Hopkins

...THEN WE'LL BEGIN.

'I've quite literally done some of my most seminal work in car parks.'

Well, now.

I hope you're not expecting as life-affirming and exciting a backstory from me as you got from Dave. Dave is very definitely the professional half of this partnership, having spent much of his life, as you've just read, writing scripts, trying to get scripts taken up, writing and writing and trying and trying and plugging away at it and doing all the right things. I, on the other hand, had never written a script in my life when Dave first suggested it. I was far too busy being *The Concrete Fox*, podcast DJ, blogger, and saviour of radio. Furthermore, I'd never read any books about how to write scripts, never even read any books of scripts. Like everything else in my life, I just always assumed I could do it if I needed to, and then put the entire subject in a box in my head and didn't think about it again (this is something I do pretty often, and I will undoubtedly refer you back to this paragraph at least once more before we're through).

But now, finally, those chickens have come home to roost, as they inevitably do. 'What chickens?' I hear you cry. 'Well,' I say, rather disappointedly, because I'm beginning to suspect you may not have been paying attention, 'metaphorical chickens, obviously.' And, with a flourish of my not inconsiderable literary skills, I pluck yet another metaphor from the language tree. They say – those people who enjoy saying this kind of thing – that the proof of the pudding is in the eating. Well, as you take spoonful after spoonful of our creamy *Hellanory,* dear listener, you are eating the proof – or not – of that particular spongy, scripty desert. With me? It is for you, not I, to comment on my flavours, and declare my humble word-puddings either fruity or flatulent. How's that?

That's writing, that is.

Anyway. My point is that Dave's a 'real writer', not me. And Dave's long journey to *Hellanory* and mine really have only two things in common. One is that the early parts of our lives were strangely parallel; born within a few months of each other, we grew up in (roughly) the same part of London, and both went to work for the much-missed Our Price Records, him in Upper Street in Islington and me in Oxford Street. We both spent a lot of time hanging around The Falcon in Camden, and we both played in bands that never quite made it, although mine never quite made it slightly more than his never quite made it (in case you find this clause confusing, what I mean is that Dave is more famous than me. Officially. That's why we always put his name first. That, and he gives me deadlegs).

The other thing we have in common is car parks. Dave does a lot of writing and editing in them, and I've quite literally done some of my most seminal work in car parks.

Writing scripts, then – new to me. Damned awkward Johnnies, scripts. Not completely unfamiliar with them, though, because what I have done is some acting. Acting was always going to be my standby, alternative career when I took a break from being an indie rock icon. I excelled in school drama productions, by which I mean I had a big mouth and kept pushing my way to the front. My first ever appearance on the boards was in *Toad Of Toad Hall*, a musical version of Kenneth Grahame's *The Wind In The Willows*, in which I played the fox. I know exactly what you're thinking right now, and I don't care whether you remember it or not, there was a fox in *Wind In The Willows*. Yes, there was. Go and look it up. When Toad is lost and alone in the forest, dressed as a washerwoman, he meets a fox. I can still remember my entire section of script, enrobed as it was in several lines of red ballpoint and highlighter and various scrawled stars and exclamation marks; it went like this.

(FOX enters R, sniffing)

FOX:
Half a pair of socks and a pillowcase short this week,

washerwoman! Mind it doesn't occur again!

(FOX exits L, sniggering)

Hot on the heels of this triumph, singing voice to the fore, I then appeared at Redbridge Town Hall in a schools' production of Britten's opera *Noye's Fludde*, or 'Noyer's Fluddy', as it was rendered in our North London schoolboy dialect. In it, I played a fox. This time, in a papier-maché fox mask I'd cooked up in my bedroom. Do you see where this is going? Short of being bitten by a radioactive fox, or perhaps having both my parents eaten by one, life couldn't have been much clearer about the path I was seemingly destined to follow.

By the way, don't worry about not remembering the fox in *The Wind In The Willows*. No-one does. I'll bet you don't remember that there was a fox in *The Lord Of The Rings*, either. Well, there was. Not a massive mover and shaker in the events of the Third Age, admittedly. Not on the level of, say, a Gandalf, or a Saruman. Or that Danish twat with the wooden face and a name like a hairdryer. But he was there. In fact, the small part played by the fox in the tale of Middle Earth is strikingly similar to the part played by the fox in the adventures of the hapless Toad. I can't be bothered to go and get the book, but the text goes something like this;

> **As it happens, there was a fox abroad in the forest that night; and he said to himself, "Four hobbits! And sleeping out of doors, too! There's some strange mischief at work behind this."**
> **And he was right, but he never found out any more about it.**

Fairly typical stuff. No-one ever celebrates the fox, no-one remarks upon the fox, or generally even remembers that he was around. But he's always there; on the sidelines, looking for trouble, sniffing and sniggering. If they wanted me to be a fox, I thought, a fox is what I would be. And concrete because I was born in concrete; as a child of the seventies you grew up surrounded by the stuff. It was a metaphor for life, if you'll forgive me growing a little dark for a second. As a child you think it will last forever, but it doesn't, it decays and crumbles in front of your eyes, before you're ready, before you've finished using it, while you're still occupying it.

So now you know. A symbol of our times, an icon of urban decay. The Concrete Fox.

My dramatic career fizzed like a mouthful of popping candy. Not the new stuff, the old radioactive stuff. Worrying that I was getting typecast as a vulpine outsider, I made the exciting leap to the role of 'Hunch-Backed Servant' in a horror spoof, a part for which I practised for hours in front of the bedroom mirror, showing already an innate affinity for Stanislavsky's 'Method'. The part, somewhat prophetically, required me to carry a severed human anatomical part in my pocket and get it out and wave it around at various points, to the rollicking laughter of the audience of dutiful mums and dads (I pointed out the irony in later years to my arresting officer, but he failed to see the humour).

And then, everything changed. By divine intervention (probably), young, hippy English teacher Mrs. Edwards took over the running of the school play, leading to what was possibly the pinnacle of my career - the key part of 'The Sweeper', the God figure in David Campton's *The Life And Death Of Almost Everybody*. The part was a big one – no sniffing on the sidelines here. The play opened with me walking onto a bare stage, alone, house lights still up, using a broom in silence until suddenly (and confusingly, as it turned out, to parents who were still discussing how soon they could get home) embarking on three pages of soliloquy; and after an hour and a half, it ended with me, still on stage, alone once more, talking until the lights went out. Most difficult of all, I wasn't playing a character. No whiskers, no hunchback. Just a bloke in an overall, on a bare stage. Theatrically, I was bloody naked, darling.

At the risk of seeming immodest, I think I can claim that my performance caused a minor ripple in the Fakenham area of North-West Norfolk's cultural ocean. The local paper breathlessly reported that 'Jonathan Smith was very good in a huge part that kept him on stage throughout the play', and, additionally, noted that 'when angry, he bears a strong resemblance to John Cleese'. How I laughed, when, in later years, my underlying sociopathic tendencies and anger management issues led to me beat my car with a big stick.

I was even accepted for drama college, sweetie, but then I fucked up my 'A' levels, and went to work in a record shop instead. After that I had few further brushes with the theatre, including a rank production of *The Crucible* in Pimlico and some horribly angst-ridden and worthy Legs-Akimbo-style piece at the appropriately named Cockpit Theatre in Marylebone. I played a young gay man who abused his partner and fucked everything that moved. As theatrical challenges go, it was hardly John Merrick.

A few years later I was asked to provide book and lyrics for a musical about the life of Oscar Wilde. I'd been blathering on to a bloke I met in a bar about what a perfect topic it was for a musical, and how I couldn't believe that no-one had ever done it, and how I could write the bloody thing and it would make millions. Irritatingly, the bloke in question was the musical director of the Tyne Theatre, and he said 'Go on then. I'll write the music.' Now, this was a copper-bottomed, cast-iron ticket to the big time. All I had to do was use my talent for songwriting and my mastery over the English language, together with the innate script-writing ability I knew I had (see paragraph one), and I could easily become a doyen of the theatre, a young maverick with a runaway hit on his hands. The hit I was always convinced it had to be, because I said so and everyone else was too stupid to do it. This man and his offer in a bar could be my all-access pass to The Big Time.

I wrote precisely one song[1] before getting bored, sleeping with his boyfriend and exiting stage left, either sniffing or sniggering. Probably both, now I come to think of it.

---

[1] *It was called* Who's That Man? *and it involved lots of people in Victorian costumes poncing up and down Piccadilly with parasols and making disapproving faces while Oscar Wilde strode through them all with a floppy rubber phallus strapped to his head. Actually, I didn't write that last bit. Shame. It would have improved it immensely.*

After that, rock'n'roll took over. Two decades of bands with names I won't recall here, but whose main purpose mostly seemed to be to cram a stereotypical ten-year rock stadium career into two years and a string of pub toilets. The most rock'n'roll it got was probably taking a taxi from Peckham to Mayfair to push a note about kidneys under Morrissey's hotel door in the middle of the night with a bloke in stilettos; the least was probably playing a gig with laryngitis to three people and a seagull with The Popguns. I never became the pop star I always knew I would, mostly because I kept seeing shiny stuff and wandering off. Never became Ian McCulloch, but I had a game of football with Pete de Freitas. Never became Morrissey, but shared best friends for a while. Never in the thick of the action, but always there. On the sidelines. Sniffing. And/or sniggering.

It was always fairly likely that I would end up as a teacher in the same way that it's always fairly likely that the next Pope won't be Jewish. Teaching is, after all, very much like rock'n'roll, in that everybody knows teachers can't possibly function without huge amounts of stimulants and/or alcohol, and, frankly, nobody much cares as long as you can still get up on stage and shake your thing. (Colloquially. Ancient teacher lore says that standing in a classroom and *literally* shaking your thing is generally inadvisble.)

Unexpectedly, for something that I always just *assumed* I'd be good at (see paragraph one), it transpired that I was *actually* good at it. Realistically, I was a shoe-in. If you're a teacher, having a big mouth and pushing yourself to the front isn't a drawback; it's your job description. If you're not at least a little bit a performer, inside, somewhere that you can access easily, then don't be a teacher. No-one will listen, and you'll end your days weeping in libraries.

Despite undoubtedly changing the course of world events and advancing the cause of freedom by equipping the eager, straining, multi-national youth of the world with appropriate language skills, the most important and exciting thing about being a teacher was meeting Dave Hopkins. I was giving a lecture on Christmas and New Year celebrations around the world, and I looked down and thought 'Oh look, that grinning idiot in the front row is nodding and making 'thumbs-up' gestures just like I would if I was enjoying a lecture. I wonder if we could create edgy yet humorous black comedy audio dramas together?' No, I didn't. Of *course* I didn't. I did, however, at the risk of being mawkish, recognise a kindred spirit, and a bond was strengthened by a shared love of black humour, 50s and 60s sci-fi and *Doctor Who*. Dave and I set the world to rights in the smoking area between lessons, and I was glad to have found someone who thought like me, and found the same things funny. Generally, when people laugh in my company there's an edge of nervousness about it.

After I left school, and Brighton, we kept in touch; and started, shyly, sending each other bits we'd written. Recognising that we were each other's biggest fans, the step to a joint product was an obvious one. We first started writing TV scripts, for an awesome series which I'm not going to talk about because someone might have the sense to take it up one day. And then, via our separate forays into podcasting, we had the idea – audio comedy. We arrived at it separately – I had an idea for short, two-hander sketches in my podcast, *No More Love And Flowers*, and then one day Dave came up with the idea for *Hellanory,* more or less fully formed.

I loved the idea straight away. I had fond memories of safe, cosy Jackanory from my childhood, with its 'Are you sitting comfortably?' tag line and the reassuring faces of Kenneth Williams and Bernard Cribbins and June Whitfield. It was the epitome of comfort and reassurance. Of course we should fuck it right up. Keep the format the same; fifteen minutes of first-person storytelling, but with all the comfort sucked out and slightly worried looking-over-your-shoulder discomfort piped in. It all made sense. And, somehow, it unlocked the storyteller in me; fifteen minutes was just the right length to sustain my interest and stop me getting bored and chasing shiny stuff. Besides, not that much seems shiny any more, if I'm honest.

So finally, here it is. Six plentiful helpings of *Hellanory,* for you to digest in six individual sittings, along with both the Hallowe'en and Christmas specials in all their glory, *and* a special bonus – a never-aired story about the shady origins of the many-limbed literary mammoth that is *Hellanory*. Alka-Seltzers available on request. Please love it and make us really rich, because I haven't got a pension. Thanks.

Jonathan Smith

THE SCRIPTS

- I -
THE PECULIAR CASE OF NATHANIEL FRY

Run a bath and take a dip - my metal claws will start to rip.
The sounds of frantic, desperate groaning punctuate your feeble moaning.
Your intestines spill from deep within.
Are you sitting uncomfortably?
Then we'll begin.

Dave:
Years ago, I joined an online community of writers. The general idea was that you could submit anything – poetry, short stories, screenplays, chapters of books, shopping lists – and the rest of the community would respond, give feedback or, as was the case with me, seethe with jealousy at the quality of some of the writing. I submitted a fair load of stuff, some of which, I'm sure, would have me crawling up the walls with embarrassment if I were to read it now. It was while I was a member of this community of hopeful writers that I posted up *The Peculiar Case Of Nathaniel Fry*. I was delighted with the response – over a thousand views and a load of positive comments. I felt, briefly, like J.K. Rowling.

The story itself was only a few pages long and took the form of a series of diary entries from a man who has, he believes, perfected a health-giving serum from the adrenal glands of a dog. God knows where I got that idea from but I seem to remember walking up to collect one of my kids from school and messing about with the idea of a man injecting himself with monkey serum. It was a sort of sideways step from there to get to canine adrenal glands. The finished tale was short, sweet and to the point and the story remained – and still remains, actually – one of my own, personal favourites. It never occurred to me to try and do anything else with it, or adapt it. I was happy with how it was, despite its brevity.

Then *Hellanory* came along.

Originally, I was simply going to recite the story as it stood, with various sound effects and snatches of music, but myself and Jon had agreed on a 15-minute format by that time and in its original form *The Peculiar Case of Nathaniel Fry* would barely have lasted for five. So I expanded it by adding the scene in the restaurant and suddenly the story seemed to really come alive.

The only thing that would improve it, I feel, would be if it were read not by me (I hate the sound of my own voice) but by someone like Mark Gatiss or Richard E. Grant or Paul McGann or Derek Jacobi.

Or – oh my God, yes, *yes* - Tom Baker. Tom? *Tom?* Are you there? Tom ...?

GRAMS:
Hellanory Theme Tune/Rhyme

F/X: DIDGERIDOO DRONE

NATHANIEL: (ECHOING, DREAM-LIKE)
Coronary artery disease, stroke, lower respiratory infections, chronic obstructive pulmonary disease, diabetes mellitus, Alzheimer's, dehydration as a result of diarrhoeal diseases, tuberculosis, cirrhosis of the liver ...

GRAMS:
Stone The Crows – Lazarus Hyde

NATHANIEL: (NORMAL)
Schizophrenia. Not just schizophrenia, actually. All mental illnesses, in fact. And cancer in all its varied and malignant forms. Plus heart disease, lung disease, high blood pressure, low blood pressure, kidney and liver dysfunction, ulcerative colitis, arthritis, diverticulitis, haemorrhoids, the common cold. Oh – and chilblains. I mustn't forget chilblains.

Anyway: all of the conditions I've just mentioned and, hopefully, many more human ailments gone in a single dose of an extract derived from canine adrenal glands administered via syringe into the upper thigh of a human test subject. That's the theory, anyway.

F/X: HUSHED RESTAURANT ATMOS.

A human test subject? yelps Miranda when I tell her about it all over dinner. Dinner, in fact, at a restaurant that's so expensive you have to keep turning the pages of the menu to get to the end of the long series of noughts on the prices for each main course.

It isn't the reaction I'm hoping for, in all honesty. I want her to focus on how my research will benefit mankind. How I'll win the Nobel prize for ... something or other and get the chance to tour the world giving lectures and Q and A sessions with learned types. Get interviewed on the television and radio. The inevitable autobiography. But mostly I hope that the fame and fortune resulting from my experimentation into the health-giving properties of canine adrenal extract will act as an aphrodisiac, rekindling our dwindling, ever-less-frequent sex life. But no. She chooses to focus instead, quite unreasonably in my opinion, on small details. Like the human test subject.

Er ... could you pass the salt, dearest? I ask, trying to distract her. Miranda passes the salt and puts it down firmly on the table in front of me, like she's making a move in chess. Rook to king's bishop four. Checkmate. I concentrate very hard on my plate of food. I can't meet her eye. If I meet her eye my defences will crumble.

Human test subject? she repeats. *A human test subject?*

Lovely bit of lamb, I say. *Delicious.* I can see where her line of thought is going.

She says, *I mean, who's going to be a big enough idiot to willingly have themselves injected with ...*

I glance up quickly. She's trying to pluck the correct phrase from her memory by looking round the restaurant. So I say, *Canine adrenal extract* and she says, *Canine adrenal ... whatever. I mean honestly, Natty, have you thought this through?*

Natty. Miranda insists on calling me 'Natty'. I wish she wouldn't. It's one of the few things about her that is intensely annoying and has me excusing myself at home, walking into the next room and mouthing death threats at the radiator before I can return and carry on receiving orders from her.

I don't reply and keep staring at my plate. When there's no further word from Base Camp Miranda I look up from my food, concerned. Five seconds is a long time for her to go without speaking. She's staring at me.

Natty, she repeats. *Have you thought this through, Natty?*

Clenching my fist out of sight under the table to combat the effects of her calling me 'Natty' twice in one sentence, I tell her that yes, of course I have and what's her chicken like? But instead of giving me her culinary verdict, she says *Oh God. Oh my God. Natty, no. Tell me you're not.*

And I look back up from my plate.

F/X: DIDGERIDOO DRONE

NATHANIEL: (ECHOING, DREAM-LIKE)
They all think I'm mad, of course: my fellow scientists, the researchers, the lab assistants. Even the bloody canteen staff. All of them, sniggering behind my back and, in some cases, straight into my face. Call me a paranoid nutter if you want, but I can tell by the way they all refuse to meet my eye in the lift in the morning and stare fixedly at their lentil soups and ham and coleslaw baps in the canteen at lunch times: they think I've lost it. Ha! Well. They'll be laughing on the other sides of their faces when they're sneezing germs everywhere in the depths of winter and I'm brimming with health. Or that little shit Higgins, the research fellow, the one with the bad hip. Still going to be sniggering into his fucking Macbook Pro while he's lying in a hospital bed in post-operative agony, and I'm doing back flips in front of him, shoving my superhuman health in his face as he calls the nurse for more morphine? I don't think so ...

F/X: RESTAURANT ATMOS.

NATHANIEL: (NORMAL)
Tell me you're not, says Miranda, breaking into my thoughts.

Not what? I ask, looking back at her, feigning innocence.

Miranda narrows her eyes.

You're going to do it, aren't you? You're going, she carries on, *you're going to inject yourself. With ... with ... dog ...*

Canine adrenal extract, I say. I sit upright in my chair, lay my knife and fork down on the sides of my plate, reach over the table and grasp her hands. I look her straight in the eye and it occurs to me, apropos of nothing, that I could get in a really good head butt from this position.

Miranda, I say. *I swear to you, right now, categorically, that there is absolutely no way I'm going to inject myself let alone anyone else with canine adrenal extract. Not before it's been tested thoroughly.* I give her hands an extra comforting squeeze and I eye her plate. *Now. Eat your chicken*, I say. *It's getting cold.*

I don't know why she listens to me. She doesn't usually. Maybe for once I'm so confident, so certain. Maybe it's because I don't look away from her eyes as I'm saying it. I don't know.

Whatever. She falls for it, though. Hook, line and sinker.

GRAMS:
A Singular Sense Of Detachment – Lazarus Hyde

Miranda leaves the next morning for a business trip to Cannes. I wave from the doorstep as she gets into the taxi, bound for Gatwick. She turns and watches me waving through the back windscreen as the taxi drives off and round the corner. I wonder if she's still worried, despite my assurances of the night before. And if she is worried, will she say anything to her colleagues? And how could she possibly word it? *I'm worried about Nathaniel. I think he's going to inject himself in the upper thigh with canine adrenal extract.* Even if she is worried, she'll change her tune – they'll *all* change their tunes – when she sees me brimming with health upon her return.

I realise that that suggests I'm *not* brimming with health right now, which isn't strictly true. I'm not suffering from all of the illnesses and conditions I mentioned before. I'd be in a very sorry state indeed if I was. But I have got the sniffles and a bit of a tickly throat so am what you night call under the weather.

I close the front door and ask Father what he thinks of my findings regarding the link between superhuman health and canine adrenal gland extract. He doesn't reply. He never does when I ask him things out loud. Hardly surprising. He's been dead for three years. Plus, he was a carpenter by trade so probably wouldn't have had a lot to say on the subject. But I often ask for his opinion on all sorts of matters and like to think he whispers advice in my ear when I'm unsure. And right now he's whispering *Do it, Nathaniel. Do it!*

Interesting to note that I've lived almost my entire adult life firmly believing that there's no God and no afterlife but now that I'm potentially risking my life I've started praying and talking to my dead parents. Well, parent. Of the two of them, Father would have been the one who would have listened.

As for Mother ... well. While she's not actually, technically dead, she might as well be. Licking each and every window in her nursing home every hour, on the hour, is hardly the behaviour of a sane person, is it? No wonder Father hanged himself.

Actually, there's no 'potentially' about it. I'm about to inject myself with ... well, dog juice, basically. I *am* risking my life.

Anyway. Onwards.

GRAMS:
The Light – Bernard Herrmann

F/X: DIARY ENTRY SOUND

Day one. A momentous day. Is that the right word to use? Is sticking a syringe full of canine adrenal extract into one's upper thigh momentous? Or just plain bloody stupid?

F/X: DIARY ENTRY SOUND

Day Two. Side effects? So far, none. I am, however,

experiencing a singular sense of detachment and yesterday, as I introduced Mister Thigh to Mrs Syringe, it was as if I was watching the proceedings from outside of myself. Peculiar but not necessarily unpleasant. Not wildly amusing, either, as the injection hurt like buggery. That's just a figure of speech, I hasten to add, as I have no idea what buggery feels like.

I didn't sleep much. Probably down to being totally wired by the excitement. Or because I have the adrenal gland serum of a dog coursing through my veins. I suspect the latter.

I felt an uncontrollable and unusual urge to go for a run in the park. But, like I say, apart from that, no side effects.

F/X: DIARY ENTRY SOUND

Day Three. I went for another run in the park today. But then I got distracted and chased some pigeons then ran home. I was panting like hell when I got back. Realised I was ravenous when I got in and started loudly demanding my breakfast. Don't know what I was thinking – no one was going to bring me breakfast as Miranda isn't at home and, even if she was, I doubt she'd respond to me barking at her to be fed. And I don't mean barking in the literal sense. So I ran into the kitchen, poured some cereal into a bowl and sat at the kitchen table with it. I felt weird sitting at the table but couldn't work out why. And, curiously, it felt even more weird using a spoon to eat cereal, even though I've always eaten cereal with a spoon, as have most of the cereal-eating population.

I went for a nap. I couldn't get comfortable so I dumped my duvet on the floor and slept on that, curled up.

Still no side effects, though.

F/X: DIARY ENTRY SOUND

Losing track of the days. Today I go for a run in the park. I have a quick pee up against a tree and, later, a poo in a bush.

Much to the consternation of the mothers in the children's playground. I see some of them grabbing their children and looking concerned. A few of them start speaking into their mobile phones so I run home.

It's 6.30 in the evening. I sit in the hall staring at the door, whining and waiting for Miranda to walk in as she usually does at this time. Then I remember she's in Cannes so I wee up against the sofa in protest.

No side effects yet.

F/X: DIARY ENTRY SOUND

I'm totally losing track of the days. I've been chewing the furniture and a pair of Miranda's favourite shoes. That'll teach her to go away for days on end leaving me here by myself.

I hurl myself at the front door, yelling and shouting at the letterbox when the postman makes his delivery. He won't be back in a hurry.

No side effects.

F/X: DIARY ENTRY SOUND

Ooooh, I'm a bad, bad boy. I do a poo on the living room carpet and chew a book because I want to. Miranda won't be pleased when she gets home as it's a collection of Philip Larkin's poems, given to her and signed by her father, who is equally as dead as mine. But I'll be pleased to see her. I feel an urge to lick her face and I have a strong desire for her to tickle me behind the ears.

Her flight will have landed by now but she won't be back for at least an hour and a half. I'm going to go and wait for her in the hallway.

Really want to have a run. Perhaps she'll take me to the park.

Definitely no side effects.

F/X: DIARY ENTRY SOUND

Day ... er ... Anyway. Miranda is very angry. Has been for days. Maybe it's weeks, now. Have lost track. The look on her face when she got back from ... wherever it was – Canterbury? No – Canada? No. Anyway. She got in from wherever it was and found me waiting for her in the hall with my belt in my mouth, wanting to go out. It was difficult to fathom her expression. She certainly didn't find it amusing when I followed her round the flat sniffing her arse. Also, the chewed furniture, the mauled shoes, the fact that I've been sleeping on the bedroom floor instead of in the bed and that I now choose to eat my food from a bowl on the kitchen floor without a knife and fork. All of this has made Miranda a very grumpy lady indeed. She despairs. Thank God I've been pooing in the garden and not on the floor in the flat since she got home.

She really doesn't like it when I sit by the front door shouting at her to take me out, either.

But she must be starting to forgive me. She's just told me we're going out this afternoon. I saw her put a big sack and a load of bricks in the back of the car. I asked her where we're going and I'm very excited.

She says we're going down to the river. For a *very* long walk.

GRAMS:
Not Quite Cricket – Lazarus Hyde

END

- 2 -
ORWAK BALER IS UNWELL

Come in, young stripling, don't you wail.
I bring you hither to hear a tale.
Although you wriggle, writhe and moan,
there'll be no help — you're quite alone.
So fidget not and feign to squirm,
the straps that hold you are quite firm.
So cease your struggles and stop that din.
Are you sitting uncomfortably?
Then we'll begin.

Jonathan:
Orwak Baler was the first of the *Hellanory* stories to take shape in my mind. Contrary to popular belief, the name of the protagonist is neither an anagram nor a veiled reference to some obscure sci-fi character, but rather a large cardboard-crushing machine. Oddly, perhaps, I thought the name would be ideal for a character in a story, and I married it in my mind to an idea I'd had, set in the near future, about a government spin-doctor who goes mad and decides to start telling the truth. Orwak being 'unwell' – a nod, of course, to the immortal Jeffrey Bernard - seemed appropriate, although indicating, in this case, not a state of alcoholic inebriation but a desire to tell the truth in a world of falsehoods. Also, in the end, of course, it refers to being blown up by a pair of exploding tits, an event which is virtually guaranteed to leave you feeling a tiny bit peaky.

Orwak was born, of course, out of 'TrumpDump' – that phenomenon pervading the contemporary world in which facts can be 'alternative', and the truth is negotiable. It was my original intention to make Orwak a citizen of the USA, the land that spawned Kellyanne Conway – it sounded like the sort of stupid bloody name an American would have, after all. But I decided that (a) it made the story too obviously Trumpian, and (b) the phenomenon of TrumpDump was becoming global, and, having been written in the endless denial of hope that is/was 'Brexit', there was no way that the story should let our own political class off the hook.

Also, (c), I can't do an American accent.

'Orwak Baler' was originally intended to be a kind of dark

love story – I think I had grand designs on it being a '1984' for the current age. Thankfully, I quickly realised that this was quite a twatty idea, and it would be much more satisfying – not to mention true to my gutter instincts – to marry the 'Ministry Of Truth' shizzle with a bloke dressed up as a clown and a big pair of exploding knockers. Orwak Baler, with his 'Truth Events', is an anti-hero for the Instagram age – slowly losing his grip on reality, questioning everything, and defying the authorities with blood and violence, while Joe and Joella Public look on through their smartphones and upload him onto social media. The tale is every bit as much a searing social commentary as anything written by Charlie Brooker, although – unfairly, you might think - he's very many times richer and more successful than me. And this despite being approximately the same degree of grumpy.

Netflix – get in touch. That's all I'm saying.

Finally, our Orwak had to become a clown, and he had to do so for all the reasons that he so ably described in the story. He is, indeed, descended in direct and glorious lineage from Lear's fool, speaking truth to power; but, more importantly, he is the anti-Trump. He ostensibly tries to appear a fool, while actually being serious. Whereas Trump believes he looks serious and statesmanlike, while in reality a pair of giant rubber knockers would only serve to lend him gravitas.

SIDENOTES

The line '...truth-telling knockers' at the very end is completely gratuitous, adds nothing to the monologue, wasn't in the original script, and is only included because it made me laugh. Laugh to the extent that I had to have four attempts at recording it.

There's a musical joke in this episode. Ten *Hellanory* 'clever dick' points to anyone who spotted it. Yes, the track sampled and looped beneath the first half of the story is 'Dissidents', by Thomas Dolby, a song about a rogue journalist. And before you go searching for musical jokes in the other stories, I'm not generally that clever.

The other piece of music that's heavily used is a track I composed around the turn of the century, and is constructed entirely from music sampled from porn films.

GRAMS:
Hellanory Theme Tune/Rhyme

GRAMS:
214sJC – Taking Advantage [Slo-Mo #1]

ORWAK:
It was right at the moment when my tits exploded that I knew it had all gone too far. I had never wanted this. Believe me. The crowds, the glitter, the cheers, the explosions, the multiple deaths. I never wanted any of it. It started as a giggle, really. That was all I ever wanted, to tell the truth - to have a laugh.

To have a laugh. And to tell the truth.

GRAMS:
Thomas Dolby – Dissidents (Loop)

My job did *not* involve telling the truth. Except ... well, it depends on your definition. People think truth is something that exists independently in nature, hidden in the rocks, waiting to be discovered. And it is, but not exclusively. Truth can be manufactured, too, just like socks, or watch batteries, or taramasalata. It can be pieced together from other materials, welded into an emotional amalgam at furious temperatures by dedicated, grey-faced welders. Yes, it's not as sturdy as the pure stuff. It has flaws, it has contradictions, it can fall apart if you examine it too closely. But that's not a problem – as long as you understand your market. If you understand your market, you can sell a welded-together, man-made truth much, much more easily than you can sell the real thing.

My name is Orwak Baler, and I know these things because I was one of the welders. I worked for the Department of Communications & Culture, in the section known as *Factual Understanding and Communication Facilitatory Alternatives Committee (Experimental)*. Better known to those of us who worked there by its abbreviation, FUC FACE. Early on, right at the beginning, someone pointed out that the initial letters of the department's name spelled out 'FUC FACE', and that such an outcome was so outrageously unlikely unless someone had planned it that there must be an intention from high up to make the department seem frivolous, and even ridiculous, right from the start. That way, we agreed, we could do important, deniable, revisionary work while nobody else took us seriously. The next day, we were greeted with a memo which strenuously denied that this was the case, denied, indeed, that there was a case to answer, claiming that the whole thing was fake news and that the initial letters actually spell 'BUTTERFLY', and that this had been verified by a company that made dictionaries.

It was a taste of things to come.

GRAMS:
214sJC – Taking Advantage [Slo-Mo #2]

I watch the prime minister explode in a shower of flesh. Some bits are large, some just individual liver spots, flying through the air like tiny spaceships. What I later discover to be most of his left buttock hits me in the face with a splat, just like the most perfectly-placed custard pie, obscuring my carefully-applied clown face with blood and bits of pulpy tissue. A buttock in the face makes you evaluate your life, makes you think 'how did I get here'?, particularly when it's not attached to anything.

GRAMS:
Thomas Dolby – Dissidents (Loop)

It started small. The kind of thing we had all expected. The Secretary of State for Work and Pensions had made a claim about unemployment which was all kinds of wrong; we built a supporting pyramid of studies and research which upheld it, and then put him on a self-aware Channel 4 panel show to splash it. The Defence Secretary ridiculously underestimated the number of civilian deaths in our latest Middle East endeavour; we massaged the figures, spoke to different people, found reasons to exclude certain groups, and miraculously came up with the same number he quoted.

Then we bunged the fucker on a bungee rope wearing union jack underpants during his interview. We distracted the public with one hand, while with the other we created *new truths*. And that's what they were – remember that. No lies passed through our hands. Not at first. We just... created new realities. Reality is what history says it is. And history is just what people remember, and what they believe.

And then it happened. The revulsion came first. The revulsion, then the revelation, and then the rebirth. DreGs, the Department for Rebuilding Great Britain, which was set up after BREXIT, wanted to hush up the fact that refugee children were being bussed into the country through our inadequate borders and put to work as skivvies and cleaners for middle-class families in the Tory hinterlands. We figured out that since these kids were in the country illegally, and since they weren't being paid, and they weren't on any records anywhere, then as far as anyone who mattered was concerned they didn't really exist, and so could be written off as *'Assets (Misc)'*. It was a big gamble, the biggest we'd taken, claiming that thousands of children who were blatently scrubbing toilets and shopping for granola in Hampshire *weren't actually there.* But we managed it. You fell for it. You swallowed it. You bloody idiots.

And that was when something snapped in my head, like a rubber band that had been twisted too many times. What the pimply, teenage FUCK? I was actually cancelling out people's existence, writing them out of history. I was being GOD. And not a nice God. A *twatty* God.

GRAMS:
214SJC – Taking Advantage [Slo-Mo #3]

There goes the Home Secretary, almost cut in half by one of my cleansing nipple bombs of truth, sliding over himself and slipping sideways like an anglepoise. I never did like him, he had a stupid moustache and he sounded like a horse,

F/X: FLYING BOMB SOUND THEN EXPLOSION

but I'm sad to see him die. This really has all gone too far. But what's done is done, and that's the truth. And I know, being The Clown Of Truth. I can't turn back the clock. Again, because I'm the Clown Of Truth, not fucking Doctor Who.

GRAMS:
214sJC – Wiggy (Edit #1)

I left my job, left my old identity. I became a clown, because it is the fool who is traditionally allowed to speak truth to power and remind the mighty of their fallibility. And, because the people thought their elected representitives were clowns, I thought it fit that a clown should be ranged against them. And also because I still had the clown costume I bought for Karen's fancy dress when I was trying to get off with her but it turned out she had a clown phobia so I had a wank instead, when I got home, still wearing the clown costume. Alistair Crowley used to believe that semen was power. Well, I have loads of power in my clown costume.

That's why I called myself 'The Jizzler'. That, and I thought it was funny.

And it was, at first.

I staged my first Truth Event meticulously; just as the Prime Minister stood outside Number Ten proclaiming that he did not have, nor ever had had, any dealings with dodgy dictators, I stood in front of the camera, bent over and dropped my baggy pants to reveal voluminous drawers replete with pictures culled from the archives, pictures of the PM shaking hands with a host of dodgy dealers whose human rights records were as clean as a curry fiend's ringpiece. The press loved it. The public loved it. 'Jizzler' fan clubs sprang up all over, and the headlines rolled in with every Event. 'Jizzler Strikes Again'. 'Another Faceful From The Jizzler'. 'Jizzler's Cunning Stunts'. I became the *zeitgeist*, and for a while everyone loved me. For a while I loved myself.

For a while.

**GRAMS:
214sJC – Taking Advantage [Slo-Mo #4]**

F/X: POLICE SIRENS APPROACHING. CAR SKID. STOP

The sirens are pretty deafening, now. The police will have me in a minute. It's not like I can run anywhere, reinforced plastic tits hanging from me like scooped out flesh. I'm scarred, anyway, from the Truth Shrapnel, despite the KEVLAR body suit under the costume. It's nearly over. This is where the laughing stops.

F/X: DISTANT EXPLOSION

**GRAMS:
214sJC – Wiggy (Edit #2)**

Try and remember you loved me, once. Remember The Jizzler, *your* Jizzler, photo-bombing the Environment Minister who was pledging to protect organic farming, pulling a bunch of mutated, sterile, GM broccoli, as if by magic, from his sleeve. Remember the peace conference, when the Foreign Secretary lambasted Russia for its imperialist intentions, and The Jizzler descended from the roof on a wire, pulling from his sleeve, this time, a string of flags of old colonies,

F/X: CROWD CHEERS

places we ground under our heel, places where the hatred is still ingrained like coal dust, a string that seemed to go on forever. You loved me, then.

And then it all went dark. The proclamation from the Home Office that 'no child in Britain is realistically living in poverty' was too much for me. I shouldn't have done it, but at the time it seemed right to rock up at party conference in the old car and stand there, holding the door while a hundred and thirty-six poor kids got out, scratching and limping.

F/X: CROWD BOOS, HISSES

Several of them were so ill that they didn't make it until the ambulances arrived. The wheels falling off the car was a comedic afterthought, but by that time, the laughter was fairly sparse.

The police got involved when I started throwing buckets of water over members of the Treasury, because at the last minute they always turned out to be not buckets of water at all but squares of shredded money, money I had syphoned from their own bank accounts earlier in the day. And then, of course, came the balloons filled with water, water from the 'safe' new Chinese nuclear facility, the one waved though with massive international bribes. That was when I went on the run.

It's not easy, being a fugitive truth-telling clown. Particularly because I insisted on meticulously applying my clown face, always, every morning, no shirking. The Jizzler must always be The Jizzler. You have to have standards. Otherwise you end up... well, you end up with me.

GRAMS:
214sJC – Taking Advantage [Slo-Mo #5]

They're coming, now. I can see them, running at me, waving guns. Soon, it will all be over. I hope they give me credit. They may have wiped out half of the cabinet, but my Exploding Boobs Of Truth were a work of fucking genius. Miniature cluster bombs spraying out pictures of government figures with prostitutes, with dictators, doing dodgy deals, collecting envelopes of money. All the hidden things, all the secrets, all the truth.

And glitter. Oh, and those Japanese ninja stars. The ones with razor-sharp edges.

And all this exploding from a massive, oversized pair of breasts. There's nothing that tickles the British public more than a great big pair of knockers.

Truth-telling *knockers.*

My name is Orwak Baler. I used to be a welder, and now I'm a clown. I went too far, but only because they went too far. They went way too far. It got to the point where it just.... wasn't funny.

F/X: LOUD EXPLOSION

**GRAMS:
Elizabeth Taylor – Send In The Clowns (Edit)**

over

F/X: MULTIPLE POLICE SIRENS APPROACHING. CARS, SIRENS STOP. POLICE RADIO CHATTER

END

- 3 -
SURPLUS BAGGAGE

Come in out of the wind and cold and sit down here,
if I might make so bold.
In the fire, all warm and toasty,
your shattered ribs and limbs all roasty.
In a chair, tied nice and tight,
you can't escape, try as you might.
So heat the poker, pass me my pins.
Are you sitting uncomfortably?
Then we'll begin.

Dave:
Surplus Baggage wasn't always the piece of finely-crafted audio perfection as you hear it presented in *Hellanory*. It started out life as a short story, published in the *Someone Has To Die* crime anthology, compiled from entries for a competition organised by the wonderful and sadly long-since-defunct writing website *Spike The Cat*.

I've forgotten how I came up with the idea of an elderly female assassin doing bad deeds on behalf of her local Town's Women's Guild but I suppose that doesn't really matter. What does matter is that having written it and having had it published – a rare moment of success accompanied by a cheque for £50 - I never really forgot the idea and always felt that it could go on to greater things. Over the years – and it's been a good fifteen or so since I wrote the original – I've reworked it many times. It became a half-hour film script, a radio play, the basis of a probably wisely-abandoned novel and, more recently, an episode of an anthology TV series that me and Jon worked on for a bit, the details of which I won't reveal as the idea for the series is a good one and we could well return to it in the future. Possibly.

When Jon and I started batting ideas for *Hellanory* across the badminton net of audio drama, we hit upon the hilarious wheeze of Jon's mum Mollie being the voice behind the rhymes at the beginning of each episode – a task to which she subsequently took with admirable gusto. Hearing her intoning *Are you sitting uncomfortably? Then we'll begin* ... led to me rewriting *Surplus Baggage*. I sent the script to Jon but realised that it was a bit much to expect his mum to record something of that length. Introductory rhymes of less than thirty seconds were one thing, but a whole fifteen or twenty minutes were a huge ask. Or so I thought. And, initially, so did Jon. He said 'Leave it with me and I'll see what I can do.' So I promptly forgot about it and started writing something else instead.

Three weeks later, and unknown by me at the time, Jon and Mollie, in a mad, day-long fit of creativity, the sneaky devils, came up with *Surplus Baggage* as you hear it in *Hellanory*. Jon sat hunched over the controls and directed the recording while Mollie did the speaking. I'm not exaggerating when I say that listening to it for the first time was a bit of an emotional moment for me. Quite a bit of an emotional moment, actually, as it was the first time I'd ever heard someone else speaking words that I'd written. Mollie literally breathed life into Edith Cooper, the aforementioned assassin. I found myself laughing out loud with joy upon hearing her deliver lines that I'd only previously heard, in my own voice, in my own head. And the moment when she spat out the words *not sucking it through a ... a fucking straw* honestly raised goosebumps on my arms and does so every time I hear it. I couldn't quite believe how professional and thoroughly immersed in the role she sounded. Jon bought her the biggest cake he could find as a reward.

So thank you, both, for making *Surplus Baggage* what it now is. Mollie, your vocal talents and Jon, your sensational efforts behind the recording console soared majestically above and beyond all expectations. I can't really put into words quite what your combined efforts in the name of *Hellanory* mean to me but I've had a bloody good stab at it. I will be eternally and rightfully grateful to you both. I raise a glass of something alcoholic in your general direction for coming up with what is absolutely the definitive version of *Surplus Baggage*.

SIDENOTES

Here's an interesting fact. In the opening rhyme, the last line as I originally wrote it was *Your head a metal hood is in. Are you sitting uncomfortably? Then we'll begin*. But when it came to recording it, Jon substituted the line for *So heat the poker, pass me my pins* ... which I think is a far superior line.

He also changed the order of the music around because he thought it worked better that way but mainly, as he admitted, to annoy me.

The rotter. I'll get him back for that, just you see.

GRAMS:
Hellanory Theme Tune/Rhyme

F/X: TEA ROOM BACKGROUND

EDITH:
Mrs Bryce arrives bang on time and sits opposite me at our usual table in the corner.

Ah, Hilary, I say cheerfully, by way of greeting. *I thought I sensed a disturbance in The Force.* But it's clear she doesn't get the reference. She studies, pointlessly, the sheet of badly-typed, light-blue A5 paper that passes for the menu at The Mousehole Tea Rooms.
The prices have gone up, she intones.
I smile back at her.
Really, Hilary, I say. *Do we have to go through this every time? I know who you are, you know who I am, so ...*
Mrs Bryce glares with undisguised hatred across the table.
The prices have gone up, she repeats. I note the irritation in her voice and can only hope that it will lead to something far more serious and life-threatening.
But I hear their toasted tea cakes are wonderful, I reply and Mrs Bryce smiles with grim satisfaction, always a stickler for correct procedure.
Edith, she says.
Hilary, I reply.
She places the menu aside and fixes me with her cold, grey eyes.
Now. The Town's Women's Guild are in need of your ... assistance. She speaks slowly and precisely, like a James Bond villain. *They need to arrange another ... coffee morning.*
Coffee morning? I say. *So we're not calling it a jumble sale any more? Or is The Guild actually organising a proper coffee morning?*
Mrs Bryce scowls. It's not an attractive sight which is unsurprising as Mrs Bryce is not an attractive woman.
It's not The Guild, she snaps. *It's The* Town's Women's *Guild. They'd appreciate your ... input.*
I give her one of my sweet smiles. Sugar – I like to think – laced with arsenic.

I'm loving the heavy emphasis on the last word of your sentences, Hilary, I say. *Like a James Bond ... villain. "No, Mister Bond. I expect you to die."*

The old hag doesn't smile back. The last recorded instance of her face cracking was in 1976, but the details are unconfirmed.

Very amusing, Edith, she says.

Well I certainly try, I say to her. *Now then. The jumble sale.*

Coffee morning, she snaps.

Sorry. Coffee morning. Can I ask who will be ... hosting? Christ. She's got me at it now.

Mrs Bryce puffs herself up, trying to make herself look important.

My role within the Town's Women's Guild, she says, *is - as you know full well, Edith - solely messagerial. I have no part in the decision-making process. My job is to pass on your acceptance, or otherwise, of the ... task.*

You very nearly said mission then, didn't you? I say.

Mrs Bryce takes a deep breath. It's a pity it's not her last.

Do you accept, she says, *or not?*

I sip my tea.

I accept, I say, *on one condition.*

Mrs Bryce frowns, looking confused.

I smile gently at her. *I know it's a big word, Hilary, but do try and keep up.*

Mrs Bryce's hand clenches into a fist on the table and she looks like she's about to say something, so I carry on speaking and don't give her the chance.

I want you to give The Guild - sorry, the Town's Women's Guild - a message, I say.

I'm not a messenger, she says, tartly.

Even though your role is a solely messagerial one? I ask.

She takes another deep breath.

What is it?, she asks.

This is the last time, I say. *The last one. It's time they found someone else.*

Well, this is very ... irregular, she states. The pompous cow.

I raise an eyebrow, like Mister Spock.

Irregular? I say back to her.

Mrs Bryce smiles, icily.

It's a big word, Edith, she says. *Try and keep up.*
I return the ice.
Oh, very good, Hilary. Touche. Now, pass the message on. There's a good doggie.
Mrs Bryce controls herself. Just. She glances around furtively and opens her handbag, reaching in.
Very well, she says. *Here.* For a moment, I think she's offering to pay for my tea. But no. She pulls out an A4 envelope and places it on the table, sliding it across towards me with an arthritic finger.
You'll find full details of the ... coffee morning there. In the envelope.
Oh goody, I reply.
Mrs Bryce gives me a self-important sniff.
I must get on, she sniffs.
I say, *Oh, are you going, Hilary?* My voice drips with as much fake disappointment as I can muster. *That's a shame. You won't stay and join me in a little something? The cream teas really are to die for.*
But Mrs Bryce ignores me.
Please let the Town's Women's Guild know, via me, when everything's en ... actioned, she says.
Yes, Meester Bond, I reply in a foreign accent. Then I realise what she's said. *I have to confirm via you? That's not normal procedure.*
Mrs Bryce gives me an I-know-something-that-you-don't sort of a look.
No. Indeed. Things are changing, Edith, she says. *The Town's Women's Guild are making efforts to ... streamline their operation. Out with the old and in with the new. They're stripping it all back. Cutting out the rubbish. Getting rid of surplus baggage.*
Yes, yes, I snap back at her. *I know what streamlining means, Hilary.*
So, she says. *When the task is ... concluded, you will come to my house and confirm. Back entrance.*
Well, well, well, I think. Back entrance, is it? Hilary. You dirty old devil.
Mrs Bryce looks me up and down one last time and then pushes back her chair, gathers her handbag and leaves the table, trying to walk away like Darth Vader sweeping through the room. Her recent hip operation —which, unfortunately,

she survived- makes this difficult.

I pick up the envelope. It contains, as usual, a sheet of A4 paper, folded in half, then into quarters.

I unfold it carefully and there in the bottom left hand corner is a name.

GRAMS:
Mr Parker Loses His Footing – Lazarus Hyde

Eileen Hendry calls me the next morning while I'm having breakfast and reading *Empire* magazine. Eileen is about the nearest person in the whole of Thatchwood that I could come to calling a friend. She's like a cross between Margaret Rutherford and Hattie Jacques and speaks so loudly that I sometimes wonder why she bothers phoning. She could just shout the arrangements and I'd hear her from five miles away. She comes here every week, without fail, and always brings the nicest cakes. I arrange to meet her at four after I've ... well, arranged the coffee morning.

But before that I have things to do. I walk into town and into the library. I look for something for Reg but I can't find anything he'd like. In the end I go and speak to Mary behind the desk. She's nice enough, but nervous and fluttery.

Hello, Edith. And how are we today? Keeping well? she asks in that way that people do when you've reached your seventies and they think you either can't hear or have lost your brain somewhere along the way.
Oh ... you know, I reply. *The usual aches and pains.*
Can I help at all? She asks this for the benefit of the handful of other customers in the library.
Yes, I think you can, I say. I lean in a little closer and bring my voice down low, just above a whisper. *I need to organise a coffee morning.*
Mary, in an equally low voice, says *You were here all afternoon. If anybody should ask.*
Thank you, dear, I mutter. Then in my normal voice, *Thank you, Mary. That's very helpful.* I don't think anyone else in the library is actually listening, but you can never be too careful

and I pride myself on being professional at all times.
I cast an eye around the library.
I couldn't find anything he would like, I say. I surprise myself when I say this. I wasn't intending to. It's just sort of ... well, popped out, I suppose.
Who, dear? Mary asks.
Reginald, I say.
Mary looks confused.
I mean, it's all right, I say. *I've still got one to finish for him.*
Mary is frowning and looking concerned.
She says, *Are you ok, Edith?*
It was a year ago. Today, I say. Again, I say this without really thinking. *And this is the first time, in a year, that I haven't been able to find anything he'd like.*
Mary is now concerned and confused in equal measures.
I thought ... the books ... were for you, Edith, she says.
I shake my head vaguely. *No. For Reg. I read them to him.*
Mary's eyes move from side to side, looking for a way out of the conversation which is, it would appear, slightly more than she bargained for.

Every Wednesday, I was in there for him. Choosing his books. He always let me choose his books. You know what I like, Edie, he'd say. Used to get so irritated if I got him a book he'd read before, though.

(SUDDEN ANGER)

That ... that *bloody* stroke.

I was there. With him. In Harper's. Waiting while he tried on a pair of trousers in the fitting rooms. The last thing he said to me was *I'll try 'em on. Check my arse, Edie, and tell me what they look like.* And he went into the fitting room, pulled the curtain and - *bang!* The stroke. Right out of the blue. Found him in there. Unconscious. Trousers round his ankles, socks up to his knees. One moment he's an active, healthy, fun-loving man. Then ... that was that.

Couldn't do any of the things he used to love after that.

Walking. Talking. Eating food with a knife and fork. Not sucking it through a … a *fucking* straw. Just sitting there, all day long, in that chair, day after day after day after … day. Staring at me, staring at the television, staring out of the window. Always staring.

And dribbling. Staring and dribbling. Staring and dribbling.

F/X: HEARTBEAT. LOUD, ECHOING

That's what killed him in the end. The stifling boredom, being trapped inside a body that didn't work any more. That and the pillow I held over his face until he'd stopped breathing.

F/X: HEARTBEAT - LOUDER

GRAMS:
Dirtball – Lazarus Hyde

The back door opens as far as the chain will allow and Mrs Bryce peers through the crack.
Avon calling, I say, cheerfully.
Mrs Bryce's eyes narrow in what she probably thinks is a warning glare but in fact she manages instead to look like she wants to go to the toilet.
I sigh.
The prices have gone up, I say.
Say it properly, she hisses.
I roll my eyes up to heaven.
I see the prices have gone up, I say.
But I hear their toasted tea cakes are wonderful, says Mrs Bryce and opens the door, but only just enough to let me through. I step in.
Honestly, Hilary, I say. *That line doesn't even make sense. It's completely out of context. Have a word with the Guild, will you?*
Mrs Bryce shuts the door.
It's the Town's Women's Guild, she snaps. *Follow me please. Living room.*
Mrs Bryce leads the way into the room at the front of the

poky house and installs herself in a high-backed armchair by the crackling fire. She doesn't offer me a seat.
Delightful room, Hilary, I lie.
Thank you, she says.
I love what you've done with the wallpaper and the furniture and the carpets. And the curtains. Very retro. And that smell. Mmmm. Delightful.
Are the arrangements for the coffee morning …? Mrs Bryce falters, her eyes moving quickly left and right as she searches for the right word.
I raise my Mister Spock eyebrow.
In order? I offer. Mrs Bryce gives me one of her sniffs. I carry on. *Yes, they are. You can pass the message on.*
Mrs Bryce sniffs again.
Excellent. Excellent. The Town's Women's Guild will be … delighted.
I take another look around the room.
I don't suppose there's any chance of a cup of tea, is there? I ask.
Mrs Bryce smiles grimly and picks up a newspaper from where it lays folded on the arm of her chair.
No, she says. *There isn't.*
I imagine pouring scalding hot tea over Mrs Bryce's head while she feigns deep interest in the headline on the front page of the paper.
You'll see yourself out, she adds, without looking up.
Yes, I say. *Yes I will.*
I turn slowly on my heel and walk towards the door, passing the armchair as I do so. I stop just behind the armchair and jab my thumb into the nerve cluster at the base of Mrs Bryce's skull. Mrs Bryce's head jerks up for a moment before she slumps forward, unconscious. I pull the cushion out from behind Mrs Bryce's back then ease her backwards so that her head is resting on the back of the armchair and acknowledge the feeling of pride at a job well done. Mrs Bryce really hadn't seen that one coming.
Goodbye, Hilary, I say.

I hold the cushion over Mrs Bryce's face for two minutes, listening to the ticking of the grandfather clock in the corner and the crackling of the fire in the fireplace. I look at the offensive curtains and the violent carpet and calculate that the house must have last been decorated in 1972.

When it's done, I replace the cushion behind Mrs Bryce's back and take out the envelope that she gave me yesterday. The envelope that had a sheet of paper with the name Hilary Bryce printed in the lower left hand corner. I wonder what she'd done to annoy the powers that be at the Town's Women's Guild. It was probably something completely innocuous, like over-buttering a crumpet at a monthly meeting. Or it might have been that her recent hip operation had made her less effective in other people's eyes. I'll probably never know. No one ever really tells me anything other than who. And where to turn up.

I throw the envelope into the fire and watch it burn. Then I leave and walk to the telephone box on the corner of the street.
The voice that answers is snooty and Scottish.
Hello, it says.
One less for the coffee morning, I say.
I'm very sorry. I think you have the wrong number, comes the usual reply and the line goes dead.

It will take me about ten minutes to walk home from here. I know that by the time I arrive, the necessary arrangements will have been made. Someone will have called in on Mrs Bryce and found her dead in her living room, then made a phone call to Doctor Winslett who will pronounce her dead from a heart attack, just like he has done with all the others. Doctor Winslett has no real choice in the matter. On the few occasions when he has objected to medical forgery, the Town's Women's Guild have felt the need to remind him, discreetly, about the photographs of him and young Ivy Timcott that they have in their possession and the damage that could be caused to both his career and his personal life should they ever fall into the hands of the *Thatchwood Gazette*. The shock of that would probably kill his frail and sickly wife. *Sorry Doctor Winslett*, they will have said. *But our hands are tied. Much like young Ivy Timcott's in the photographs.*

GRAMS:
Stare Up – Lazarus Hyde

As I open the front door I'm aware of footsteps coming up the path behind me. I turn and there she is. Eileen. Vastly overweight, a voice like a foghorn and a smile so wide it blocks the path.

Ah, Edith, she booms. *There you are. How are you dear?*

I note the cake box at the top of her bag. Almond Fingers, I bet.

I stand aside to let Eileen in.

Go straight through into the living room, dear, I say. *I'll get the kettle on.*

No, you have to come in the living room first, says Eileen excitedly. *I have some rather interesting news for you.*

I smile. Eileen is a great one for gossip. I follow her into the living room and hear the door close behind me. I turn. Eileen is standing in front of the living room door, barring the way out with her bulk. The huge smile has gone. And all becomes starkly clear.

I sigh.

No gossip, then? I say.

Eileen gives a small, sad smile.

No, dear, she says, with real regret in her voice. *I'm so sorry. But orders are orders, I'm afraid.*

Eileen. You treacherous bitch, I say.

I'm ... I'm really terribly, terribly sorry, Edith.

I look her up and down. The first-class, top-of-the-range, back-stabbing ...

Direct orders from the Guild, I'm afraid, she says.

The Town's Women's Guild, I snap. *Get it right.*

It's really nothing personal, Edith.

I pull a face. *Except ... it is, really, isn't it, Eileen?*

She says, *The Guild ...* and I give her look ... *the Town's Women's Guild are streamlining their operation. Getting in new blood, throwing out the old ...*

Yes, yes, I say. *I know all about that.*

I remember Mrs Bryce's words to me in the tea rooms yesterday. *Out with the old*, I think, slipping smoothly into a defensive stance as Eileen advances slowly towards me, her

clenched fists the size and colour of cooked hams.
Out with the old and in with the new …

GRAMS:
Limu Limu Lima – The Real Group

END

- 4 -
THE BOX

Come in, my childer, settle down.
Don't cry or bleat or sob or frown.
A tale I have, which may be soothing,
and iron clasps to stop you moving.
Your ears are open, this I know;
I pinned them back an hour ago.
Your eyes are safely in this tin.
So if you're sitting uncomfortably
Then we'll begin.

Jonathan:
I had the idea for *The Box* while sitting outside my greenhouse, watching the birds. I started thinking *what if all those birds were actually exact cybernetic copies of themselves?*

No, of course I didn't. That's a complete lie. I don't know how the idea came into my head, unless I'd been thinking how nice it would be to sit outside my greenhouse all the time, and send a robot version of me to work. But I don't think so. I think it just landed from nowhere, like ideas often have a habit of doing. *One day, we won't have smartphones, we'll all have computerised clones*, I thought to myself. Like you do.

Then came the title. Immediately I knew it was very important that the Box should be the central figure in the story. The Box is the great leveller, a kind of twisted *deus ex machina*. By elevating the Box to the starring role, the lesser characters become interchangeable. And so I sat down outside the greenhouse and wrote the story, while blackbirds pecked around my feet. Around my feet, you notice. They didn't actually peck my feet. This is Norfolk, not Jurassic Park.

As often happens with stories, I wasn't entirely sure myself where it was going until about halfway through. Which gave me a problem. When I realised that the much-anticipated cyborg had actually usurped his owner's position, and was, in fact, narrating the story himself, I then had to go back through the story and deliberately remove any bits which contradicted this. Now, if any of you are as unremittingly anal as myself, you will already have done this, and might well be about to raise some objections. These, my noble Lords and Ladies, I have already anticipated, and my reply is thus: given that the android – sorry, 'cyborg' – is fitted with all of the purchaser's memories up to the point of its creation, it is then perfectly acceptable for it to refer to anything that happened 'pre-Boxing' as its own memories. And all the references to identity 'post-unwrapping' have been rendered wilfully ambiguous. So there.

The Box was the last of my three stories for the original series of six, and it did occur to me that it meant I'd set two of them in a kind of near-future, boring suburban dystopia. Unwilling to become typecast, I fully intend that *Hellanory season two* will contain at least *one* story set in medieval times. And possibly one in space.

SIDENOTES

The choice of the closing music was one of the most difficult things about recording *The Box*. I'd had it in mind ever since deciding on the title that I should use the immortal Fad Gadget single of the same name. However, for some reason, The Jam's *But I'm Different Now*, from *Sound Affects* came into my head, and the more I thought it through, the more I realised the words were perfect. Plus, it's a terrific song. But there was something about the stifled hopelessness of Frank Tovey's post-punk classic that kept dragging me back – so I decided to go with my original idea. *First thought, best thought,* as the beat poets used to say, probably following it up with *daddio*, or *cat*.

The problem arose when I sat down with my copy of *The Box*. I'd forgotten how much of it was clanky repetition, excellent when you have five minutes to spare to listen to the whole thing, but utterly useless as a 'closing titles' kind of a track. A frustrating afternoon was then spent editing the track down into what eventually became a spliced-to-hell minute and a half version. I was doubly pleased to notice that, post-splice, the remaining words could almost have been commissioned for the story.

Up yours, Paul Weller.

GRAMS:
Hellanory Theme Tune/Rhyme

GRAMS:
OMD - 2nd Thought (Loop)

COLIN:
It's two months since the box turned up. Honestly, you should have been there when it arrived. Quite the event. There was a laughing, cheering crowd outside to welcome it, like a guard of honour either side of the garden path as the delivery people carried it up to the door, to be signed for with great ceremony and more cheering. There wasn't exactly flags or bunting, but the whole thing kind of gave that impression. Dennis from around the corner kept grinning and giving me the double thumbs-up sign, Arabella was whooping, the kids were doing a little dance they'd made up for the occasion. Several people were clapping. You'd have thought I'd won the Nobel prize, or an Oscar, or something.

I should point out that this sort of thing doesn't always happen with my mail deliveries. The amused crowd of friends and neighbours had gathered because – well, frankly, because it had been such a long time coming. Not the box – the people at *MeTwo* run a pretty amazing service, and the arrival of the box was, just like in the advert, a mere forty-eight hours from my 'picking up the phone and saying hello to the new me.' No, I mean I had held out for so long – long past the time that everyone else had gone for it, slobbering at the mouth like rabid Saint Bernards. For four years I held out, four years I swore blind I didn't need one, didn't want one. Four years of being relentlessly 'out' of the 'in thing', four years of smearing scorn on the zeitgeist. Four years of arguments with Arabella, who wanted more time with me, wanted me to spend more time with the kids, imaging that being a good parent is all about quantity, not quality. Four years of 'you don't care about me', and 'you just live for your job', and even – rather unsupportably, perhaps – 'it's not *natural* to go without one'. I mean, what's 'natural' about the contents of the box is, frankly, beyond me.

GRAMS:
John Foxx – Mr. No

And so eventually I caved – for her sake, more than anything else. I caved, I gave in, I picked up the phone – and, forty-eight hours later, almost to the minute, the box arrived.

Everyone we knew had had a *MeTwo* for ages. They were rubbish at first – little more than a human-shaped cellphone or home hub. They had most of your memories, or certainly the ones that you'd recorded, but they were basically just fitted with simple algorithms, and struggled to hold a decent conversation. "Tenerife! I remember Tenerife. We had a holiday there, and you got diarrhoea". That kind of thing. Strictly for geeks. Geeks and narcissists.

Some of them even went a bit wild, like in the early days of internet bots, and started swearing like dockers or chatting about Nazis. Famously, one of them went bonkers and set fire to the house after watching a cookery programme on cable, standing in the burning wreckage, weeping wretchedly and cursing about 'pedo spinach' and global warming. But once they got the machine learning properly sorted, and the company was given legal access to your neural scans, they became the developed world's 'must-have' accessory. A cloned neural net, a ridiculously powerful processor and one of thousands of vat-grown bodies, and boom. A walking, talking computer that looked exactly like you, thought like you, but did everything you told it. The *MeTwo*. A version of you that you could send to work, install in the kitchen, or pack off out the door to do all the stuff you didn't want to do while you stayed at home and had sex with your wife, or dug the garden, or went on holiday, or had sex with somebody else's wife – or dug someone else garden. Whatever your thing was.

And for four years, while everyone else saved up and bought a *MeTwo* and then threw themselves into a bacchanalia of sex, drugs and box sets, I dug in my heels. I *like* going to work, I said. I *enjoy* my job. It gives me purpose, and makes me fulfilled. I *enjoy* spending time with my workmates. Even if they are, now, actually, cyborg versions of themselves. And, if it leaves me less time for play, well, it's all about the balance, isn't it? They used to talk about a work-life balance, back in the old days. I guess people will tell you that's what a *MeTwo* is for. To put on the other end of the scales, while you sit on the 'life' side. But I've always believed you have to balance *yourself*. The old hippies used to believe that, back in the 20th century, and they were onto something. You have to find your own balance, inside yourself. Having two of you is cheating, somehow.

They laughed at me. Of course.

GRAMS:
Bill Nelson – The Meat Room

Mostly for what they saw as my Luddite tendencies, or my out-dated work ethic, but occasionally also for my use of the term 'cyborg', which hasn't been used for about seventy years. In case you're unfamiliar, it's a term coined about a hundred years ago, at the end of the twentieth century, to indicate a mix of human and computer. 'Cyb' for 'cyber', and 'org' for 'organic', or 'organism'. Horribly archaic, of course, and conjures up images of those daft old sci-fi films. But it does pretty much sum up the *MeTwo*, and, hell, I like it. It's a good word. I'm bringing it back.

So, anyway. Where was I? Ah, yes. The arrival of the box. I must put my hands up here and say, in all honesty, that once the box was unpacked and everything was set up and turned on, I was really impressed. The cyborg was a perfect facsimile. I was looking a perfect copy of myself in the face, and it was kind of disturbing. I tried a few test conversations to check its memories, and so on – like you do – and I was amazed to discover that not only were the memories correct in every detail, but that so were the emotions and attitudes associated with them. It was, for all intents and purposes, *me* answering. I was, I must say, hugely impressed.

I actually found quite quickly that I really enjoyed talking to myself. I was pleased to find out what a nice bloke I was, to be honest. Very friendly and forthcoming. And then the hilarity began, as people tell you it always does. Arabella, who was laughing and hopping up and down like a ten-year old at Christmas, started stroking both our cheeks and getting all sexy, saying "I could take you both to bed tonight", to which the other me replied "I'm not quite sure how I'd feel about that", and we all laughed. "I'm not quite sure how I'd feel either", I said, and we all laughed again. Actually, this was all a bit rich, if you ask me, since Arabella's had a *MeTwo* for two years, but I haven't see much of it clothed, let alone naked, because she puts it back in its box, on charge, as soon as it gets in from work. It was a bit innapropriate, too, I thought, seeing as how apparently the name was originally used for some kind of feminist movement. Ho hum.

I was the one who went to work, of course. Like I said, I enjoy my job. I don't want to be stuck at home all day with Arabella, lovely as she is. Work is an experience, and I feel that you should have as many different experiences as you can. It was my counterpart, my new other half, who stayed at home. Since we were interchangeable, it didn't seem to matter which way round we worked it. And imagine my smugness when it seemed that things weren't quite as rosy as Arabella had imagined. I could tell that the other me was getting on her nerves, whining and complaining about wanting to go to work, and getting in her way, spoiling her routine. They tried to do some of the things that there was never time to do together before – that *is* the idea, after all. The pictures, the theatre, an art gallery – all they seemed to do was bicker. I couldn't resist rubbing salt into the wound a little by returning home from work after one of these flops with tickets to a West End musical and a reservation at a posh restaurant, where we both had a wonderful time, and after which I took Arabella to bed and made several kinds of very interesting love to her. Beat *that*.

I may be wrong – of course I'm wrong – but I would swear

that I could hear soft curses and mutterings coming from the box. Sometimes, I have a very vivid imagination.

GRAMS:
Henry Salomon – Love Theme *from* **Romeo & Juliet**

We stuck it out for another six weeks. I tried to hide my pleasure that the whole venture wasn't working out, but it didn't really matter anyway. Something about having the other me around has brought Arabella and I indescribably closer, we can both feel it. There's a new energy in our home now, but it's not the spare, it's me, and her. It's between *us*. Having my doppleganger around for a few weeks has let us discover each other, all over again. For me, it's like I'm seeing her for the first time. And as for Arabella, she says I have a new energy, a new dynamism, a new lust for life. And she's right, I do. She says I'm a new man. And she's right.

So there were no regrets *at all* about the experience. We're both really glad it happened. It's given us both a new chance at life together. But once we'd realised that, we also realised that we didn't *need* another me. I'm all she needs to make her happy, she says, and vice-versa. Definitely. That's how I've felt, I told her, since the first time I laid eyes on her.

So, after a lot of discussion, we put my replica back in the box, and, just like the advert, I phoned *MeTwo* and told them that I wasn't completely satisfied, and twenty-four hours later they came and picked up the box.

Like I said, they run an excellent service. The delivery people were very nice, and didn't quibble at all when they came to collect. The company will probably contact us again when the drivers get back to the depot, because we had a little trouble getting my other half back in the box – isn't that always the case? - and there were a few rips and tears here and there in the packaging. Of course, it didn't have an 'standby' switch, but I think I managed to turn it off without any of the juice leaking out.

Sadly, by the time the phone rings, Arabella and I will be in Texas, because she's always wanted to go, and I've never taken her. Never taken her *before*. But like I think I said... I'm a new man.

GRAMS:
Fad Gadget – The Box (Edit)

END

- 5 -
MY NAME IS MICHAEL CRANE

Run and hide, you won't get far.
You're on foot, I'm in a car.
Lungs a-gasping as you feel
my Renault ready for the kill.
The bumper snaps your brittle shins.
Are you sitting uncomfortably?
Then we'll begin.

Dave:
For ages – years, actually – I'd been toying with the idea for a story in which the narrator has to constantly give their name for various reasons, none of which I'd ever seriously thought about. I thought it would be fun to then end the story with the narrator saying that their name wasn't, in fact, the one they'd been giving people. I had no clue as to why this would be the case and what would happen in between the opening and closing lines, but the idea sat bubbling away in the back of my mind, like my grandmother's suet pudding wrapped in a tea towel, until it came time to write *Hellanory*.

I originally intended Michael Crane himself to be an assassin but as I'd already come up with a story about an assassin – namely *Surplus Baggage* – I thought that two in one series was overdoing it a bit. So Michael Crane became a serial killer, which I decided not in a flash of white-hot inspiration as I paced my oak-walled, book-lined study but while I was actually staring out of the bathroom window, thinking about something else entirely. Which is, now that I think about it, how most of my ideas come to me. Not always staring out of the bathroom window, of course, but generally when I'm doing something else like driving or hoovering the stairs or hiding the bodies.

The narrator was originally going to be called Dennis Tarbuck for reasons so dull that I've long since forgotten them. But the name didn't quite fit and I found that I couldn't get going with the script until I had a name that felt right. Dennis Tarbuck then changed to Alan Seedly, then Jonah Carmichael then Derek Hartley, all of which were wrong. I figured that the narrator's name had to be one that both the people populating the story and the listeners would be able to remember, without it being something outlandish and improbable like Buck Zeppelin or Dirk Rimshot. Then, out of nowhere, probably while I was walking the dog but definitely *not* while I was staring out of the bathroom window, I came up with Michael Crane. As Jon pointed out, the name opened the gateway for all sorts of comic opportunities, which I merrily chose to ignore. It was also perfect for the rather sinister purposes of the increasingly creepy narrator whose real name, of course, we never actually discover.

My Name Is Michael Crane was written entirely for *Hellanory*, rather than it being an adaptation of previous work as is the case with *Surplus Baggage* and *The Peculiar Case of Nathaniel Fry*. If I ever got stuck while I was writing it – and I didn't really, not once I'd properly got going – I would fiddle around with ideas for the backing music which is an important element in all of the episodes in *Hellanory*. This seems like a pointless thing to say, seeing as *Hellanory* is a series of mini audio dramas. Of *course* the backing music is an important element.

Sometimes, though, it's worth pointing out the bleeding obvious.

GRAMS:
Hellanory Theme Tune/Rhyme

F/X: ECHOEY ATMOS

MICHAEL:
My name is Michael Crane ... My name is Michael Crane ... My name is Michael Crane ... My name is Michael Crane ... My name is Michael Crane ...

GRAMS:
In The Cupboard – Lazarus Hyde

MICHAEL: (RELAXED AND CASUAL)
My name is Michael Crane. I'm forty-two years old. I'm a divorced father of two children. A boy and a girl. My daughter – Millie – is 13. She loves street dance and performing at competitions and my son – Louie – is 15. Other than playing increasingly dark and violent games on the Xbox that I regret ever allowing him to have and avoiding revising for his GCSEs, Louie has yet to find a passion of any kind in his life. Frances, my ex-wife, the kids' mother, stresses about this. She stressed about Louie when he was young and didn't speak til he was nearly two and a half and she stresses about him even more now.

I keep all of this in mind and repeat it to myself, like a mantra. It's important I remember the details, even though I might never have to use them. Like a writer knowing where their characters went to school, or what size shoes they wear or the colour of their underwear.

My name is Michael Crane. I'm forty-two years old. And I'm about to go speed-dating ...

GRAMS:
Jazz Pig – Lazarus Hyde

I see the advert for the speed-dating event advertised in the listings for a local, trendy cinema stroke venue, which has a bar for pre-film drinks. Apart from the cinema itself, they have a kind of function room which they rent out and it's here that the speed dating events take place. And these events are perfect for my ... well, requirements.

I phone the number listed and speak to a woman called Jennifer. She organises the events with her husband, Tony. I make a mental note of Tony's name. Tony. Anthony. Tony. I store it away for future use. I tell her that I want to come along for the event and she asks my name.
Michael, I say.
Okay, Michael, she says. *That's great. And ... your surname?*
Crane, I say. *Michael Crane.*
There's an awkward pause. I smile down the phone at Jennifer.
I know, I know, I say. *My parents were big fans.*
Big fans of what? she asks, innocently, but I know what she's thinking.
Big fans of Michael Caine, I say. *With a surname like Crane, my mum and dad couldn't resist the opportunity when I came along. So – Michael Crane it was.*
Jennifer laughs, relieved, no doubt, that I've been the one to say it and not her.
You must get a lot of that, she says and I laugh back at her.
I'm sort of oblivious to it now, I say.
Jennifer says that she looks forward to seeing me in a fortnight's time and that it promises to be a great event. Her and Tony have organised speed dating before with great success, she says.
Any marriages? I ask and she chuckles.
Just one, but it looks like there's another one on the way, she says.
I live in hope, then, I reply, and say goodbye.

GRAMS:
Out Of The Cupboard – Lazarus Hyde

I have two weeks to prepare for the event, two weeks which I spend by chatting myself up in the bathroom mirror, preparing my opening lines and how-are-yous and what-do-you-dos, accompanied by warm but slightly nervous smiles.

My first attempts result in deranged rictus grins so I tone it down and practice until I can deliver a slightly lopsided, ironic, and at the same time slightly sad grin at will without looking like a killer clown.

I'm watched over during all this by my then twenty-one year old mother. She's gazing out at me from the black and white photograph blu-tacked to the wall next to the mirror. She stares at me with those fantastic eyes, the very same ones my father said were the first thing he ever noticed about her. *You can tell a lot about a woman from her eyes,* he said. *Make sure that's what you look at first. Not her tits. Never, ever the tits. They don't mean anything. Always go by the eyes.* Sound advice for a six year old. Thanks, dad.

On the evening of the event, I shower for a luxurious ten minutes and shave the sides of my face and neck accordingly, using a Muhle R41 safety razor with a fresh Feather blade and a sandalwood-scented, Proraso shaving cream. I use a refreshing, cool after-shave balm rather than an actual after shave as I don't want to go in smelling like a ponce's bathroom. I lightly trim the goatee that I like to think is reminiscent of Roger Delgado from Jon Pertwee-era *Doctor Who*.

I check my hair, a short but unruly mop of black curls. Then, seeing that everything is as I want it, I finally slip on the pair of square, black-rimmed glasses that make me look like a Swedish architect and nod to myself in the mirror. It's those or the round, tortoiseshell ones, but they make me look like a New York writer and I used those the last time. So it's the Swedish architect that looks back at me from the mirror. Giving me the final once over with clear, piercing blue eyes.

Everything appears to be in place.

Hi, I say, resisting the temptation to wink. *Hi. I'm Michael Crane.*

I check that the black polo neck and fresh, newly-bought

black jeans are suitably unruffled. Then I leave the bathroom, slip on the black, private eye-style mac hanging on the back of the door and head out into whatever the evening has to offer.

God, I'm good.

GRAMS:
The Hole – Lazarus Hyde

I've left myself plenty of time for the twenty minute walk into town, having made several practice runs in the two weeks beforehand. I know exactly where I'm going and how long it will take if I walk briskly. I arrive at the bar, five minutes before we've been advised to arrive, as I planned, and order a half of the sort of beer that a black-clad, goatee-wearing, Swedish architect lookalike would order.

As I turn from the bar sipping my beer with narrowed eyes, I am approached by a man and a woman in, I would guess, their mid to late thirties.
Are you here for the event? asks the woman, smiling brightly. I give her a practiced, perfectly-balanced ironic but slightly sad grin.
I am indeed, I say. *Sorry – I'm a bit early.*
Oh that's ok, she says, extending her hand. I take it.
Hi, she says. *I'm Jennifer.*
Michael, I reply.
Oh – Michael Crane? she asks.
Michael Crane, I reply, nodding. *Nice to meet you Jennifer.* The man standing next to her smiles widely and we shake hands too.
Tony, he says. *Pleased to meet you.* His eyes flick over my clothes. *Ah, Johnny Cash*, he says. I frown, puzzled. He raises his eyebrows at me. *Johnny Cash?* he says. *You know? The Man In Black?* I look back at him but I don't reply because I hate him already. There's an awkward little silence. Then, doing the worst Michael Caine impression ever, he says, *Michael Crane, eh? I bet not a lot of people know that?* And he laughs at his own joke. I give him what I hope is the sort of smile given by

someone who has spent their entire adult life fending off jokes about the similarity of their name to that of a well-known, highly-respected and fantastically well-paid actor: politely amused but, at the same time, slightly resigned and a little bit irritated. I don't know what Jennifer sees in him, but I really don't like him.

I bet you get a lot of that, he says. *You know? Michael Crane?* and Jennifer laughs too loudly.

That's exactly what I said, she says.

GRAMS:
The Man Who Wrote Another Book About Trees –
Lazarus Hyde

The bar starts to fill up with my fellow speed daters. There are fifteen men, including myself and fifteen women. I ignore the men. Some of them are chatting to each other, looking nervous, reeking of desperation. I try not to focus too much on the women. I want to go in fresh, so to speak. I can feel the eyes of some of them on me but I concentrate instead on the clipboard that I – that all of us – have been given. It contains a list of numbers – one to fifteen – down the page. Next to each number are two boxes, marked Yes and No. And under the yes and no boxes is a small box marked Notes. There's only room for a couple of words, depending on the size of your handwriting. I suppose in the normal run of things, you might have, for argument's sake, say 6 out of the fifteen possibilities that you've marked with a Yes. In which case, as an aide memoire you would then insert relevant adjectives into the notes box to remind yourself of their attributes. Words like sarcastic or melodic or cautious, presumably.

I won't need to employ adjectives as a reminder. I can see in my mind's eye my list at the end of the evening. Fourteen Nos and 1 Yes. Just the one. That's all it'll take. And it won't be difficult to choose, either.

All I'll have to do is look at her eyes. And I'll know.

GRAMS:
Half-Forgotten Daydreams – John Cameron

Number one is a definite no. Her eyes are slightly crossed and I'm put off straight away, which happens as I sit down, introducing myself. The next four minutes and fifty-seven seconds are a pointless, chattering hell and I breathe a sigh of relief when Jennifer instructs us men to move along to the next candidate.

Number two has potential. Her eyes are dark and warm and they narrow when she smiles, which she does a lot. I speak first and introduce myself. *My name's Michael*, I say. *Oooh, I do like the name, Michael*, she says, butting in. *And I do like an older man.* When she says that, I see cruelty in her eyes and I dismiss her.

GRAMS:
Robbie In Pieces – Lazarus Hyde

Number three. The least said about number three, the better. I tick the No box within ten seconds of sitting down. It's an excruciating four minutes and fifty seconds until we change round.

Number four is dead. Behind the eyes. And possibly actually dead, as she says nothing, leaving the talking to me for the entire five minutes.

Number five. Oh God, number five. I make an exception and write an adjective in the Notes section as she gabbles away. She sees me writing.
What have you written? she asks playfully, peering over. I show her. *Auxiliary?* she says. *What do you mean, auxiliary?* I shake my head.
Axillary, I correct her.
What does that mean? she asks coquettishly.
And I say, with heavy emphasis, *It means, Judy, 'relating to the armpits.'* It's an awkward, endless three minutes and twenty-three seconds until we get moved on. One minute into

number six, who I've already dismissed because her eyes suggest to me Bacardi, holidays in Benidorm and hen-dos with t-shirts, I glance back and see Judy turning her nose to the side and trying to surreptitiously give her right armpit a sniff. Our eyes lock briefly and I smile winningly.

F/X: ABRUPT SILENCE.

And then ... *then* comes number seven.

GRAMS:
Theme From A Summer Place – Percy Faith and His Orchestra

Shall I compare thee to a summer's day? Thou art ... something, something. Blah blah blah. I forget the rest. Anyway, doesn't matter. The point is ... number seven. And ok, no, I won't compare you to a summer's day. I compare you, instead, to my mother. More specifically, I compare your eyes to my mother's eyes. They're like ... deep wells of liquid velvet, into which I want to desperately throw myself and drown, luxuriously. And I want to ...

Are you okay? asks number seven, frowning. I blink, suddenly aware of where I am, where I'm sitting and what I'm doing. She's been chatting away for the last minute and I haven't been paying attention. On account of the eyes.
Sorry, I say, truthfully. *I was ... look, sorry, but can I just say ... you have amazing eyes*. I only just manage to stop myself from adding *they're just like my dead mother's*, which even I realise would be ... unwelcome in the circumstances.
Number seven melts. Not literally of course. But I can see it in her ... well, her eyes. She smiles.
What a lovely compliment, she says. *A lovely compliment from a man whose name I don't even know*. She gives me an encouraging look. *It's what I've just asked you. Twice.*
I shake my head in apology.
Sorry, I say. *I was distracted.*
She gives me a small smile.
By my eyes? she asks and I shrug, apologetically. *In that case,*

you're allowed to be distracted, she says.
I clear my throat and smile back.
My name's Michael, I say. *My name's Michael Crane.* I wait for the inevitable comment but she nods and smiles and I smile back and say, *I'm sorry, I didn't catch your name* and want to add, *I was drowning in the dark waters of your eyes* but realise this might be a bit much. She laughs. We both laugh - but it's the easy laughter of two people instinctively getting on well. She sips from a large glass of Pinot Grigio.
It's Maggie, she says. *Maggie Schmidt.*
And she gives me an ironic, lopsided, sad little smile.

GRAMS:
Walking Distance – Bernard Herrmann

I'll miss this room.

Three whole weeks I've been here. I've grown accustomed to the king-size bed, the tea and coffee making facilities, the little sachets of sugar that get replenished every two days and the fantastically uncomfortable chair by the table next to the window. It's not bad for a bed and breakfast and they gave me a discount because I paid in cash. They didn't even ask to see ID. Untraceable.

I pack my things carefully and clean the room, removing all trace of myself although while I've been here I've taken the trouble to wear surgical gloves at all times. I put the black and white photograph of my dear, darling mother back in my wallet, until the next time. The black, curly wig goes into my bag, the blue contact lenses get flushed down the toilet and I shave off the goatee with some relief. The face that looks back at me from the mirror – the shaven head, the dark brown eyes, the clean shaven chin - is vastly different from the one I've been living with over the past three weeks. Frankly, I'm glad to see the back of it.

In time, of course, someone will find Maggie, but by the time they do I'll be long gone. Whoever does find her will be in for a bit of a shock. And they'll almost undoubtedly wonder where her eyes have gone. I just couldn't let her keep them, not with them being so similar to mother's.

And maybe, *maybe,* they'll trace Maggie's demise back to the man in black with the short, black, curly hair, the goatee and the glasses that made him look like a Swedish architect. And maybe they'll find out his name. *Michael Crane?* they'll wonder aloud. *I wonder if his parents were big fans?*

But it's ok. Because I'm *not* forty-two years old. I *don't* have two children called Louie and Millie, I'm *not* divorced, I *don't* have blue eyes, I *don't* wear a goatee and I *don't* wear glasses.

And my name *isn't* Michael Crane.

GRAMS:
Walking Distance – Bernard Herrmann

Well, she says down the phone, *I think that just about covers everything. We start at 8, so if you could get here five, ten minutes early, so we can all have a little mingle, that would be great. I just need to make a note of your name?*
I clear my throat.
My name? I say.

F/X: ABRUPT SILENCE

My name ... is Tony Hankirk.

GRAMS:
You Were Made For Me (Edit) – Freddie and The Dreamers

END

- 6 -
CHAR

Come in, child, into my web of fear.
No shining knights will save you here.
Within my pantry, warm and cosy,
I keep things to reward the nosey.
My knives and scalpels, sharp and shiny,
and my Fabreze which smells all piney.
So bare your underparts, lift up your chin.
Are you sitting uncomfortably?
Then we'll begin.

Jonathan:
The initial spark for *Char* came from a close friend whose grandmother had wanted, as a parting wish, to have her ashes scattered in a canal. Despite having friends who live on a narrowboat, and despite having spent countless happy hours with them floating serenely down the Bridgewater and Aylesbury canals, I'm very much an urban decay kind of Johnny. So, instead of picturing a gentle release amid sublime stretches of leafy paradise, I immediately thought of flyovers, graffiti and filth. It's just the kind of man I am. I thought it would be both humourous and instructive to write a story in which a family's innocent attempts to scatter their elderly relative turn to disaster as what should be a reflective and sober moment is interrupted by the most inappropriate things possible (unsurprisingly, these turn out to be sodomy and narcotics, my two go-to subjects for just about everything).

The idea squatted in my brain like a potentially-amusing toad for several months, maybe a year. Perhaps more. I don't keep tabs on everything that squats in my brain. My life would be full of pointless, squatty tabs. But when *Hellanory* came along, I quickly realised that this would be the perfect opportunity to wake the toad up, and prod it to see if it would do a funny little dance. So I took the idea, along with my laptop, to Huckleberries cafe in Cromer (they do Flat Whites in different sizes, including 'huge', which is a mere £2.40) to see what, if anything, would happen. Some toads dance, some toads don't.

The first thing I realised as soon as I started writing was that the story had to be told from the point of view of the deceased. I don't know why, exactly – that was never my original intention – but the way I see it now, in retrospect, was that from the very moment I opened the laptop, Char was standing behind me, very politely clearing her throat and wanting attention. As soon as I wrote 'My name is Char' – it seemed as good a place to start as any – I completely surrendered control of the writing process. Politely, but firmly, a bit like somebody nice who's been doorstepped by a double-glazing salesman, Char just took over and told her story - bumming, ganja, geese and all.

So don't blame me. I was merely a conduit.

SIDENOTES

The passage where Char floats down the canal is simply my favourite sixty seconds of anything I've ever written or recorded. It was, for me, one of those occasional, glorious moments where everything comes together. When I thought of Char in her capsule, bobbing gently on the peaceful waters, I knew instantly that the only music that would do was the old *Horizon* theme, Eno's *Another Green World*. That, married with Char's matter-of-fact commentary, just got me to exactly where I wanted to go.

Predictably, I knew, and indeed know, nothing whatsoever about *Paw Patrol*. All I know is that it's a bunch of dog cops, and that kids everywhere are crazy about it. Now, it's always dangerous, referencing something you know nothing about. But it was the correct contemporary reference, and I decided to just wing it. Having since seen an episode of *Paw Patrol*, I realise I missed the point of the programme entirely, which is not about chasing animal criminals, but (predictably) being tolerant and supportive of each other and being the best you can be. Undeterred by this howling error, I still continue to shout 'evil geese!' at any geese I happen to see on my travels, because it makes me laugh, and at the end of it all that's the only real reason I do anything.

GRAMS:
Hellanory Theme Tune/Rhyme

GRAMS:
Birddog – Country Feedback (Loop)

CHAR:
The very last thing I remember is fingers tugging impatiently at the ribbon, and then the look of surprise on the young policewoman's face as I accelerated towards her. After that, nothing. After that... just being trapped here, in my last moments, as I fade away altogether. Before that... well, before the nothing there was *something*, and before that, there was me.

My name is Char. Or, rather, I should say it *was*, what with me being dead and all. I died in a rather silly accident in the front garden - I was inspecting moss on a gnome when Tim reversed over me. I always told Tim he'd have the head off one of my gnomes with his reversing, but in the end it was my pancreas. Dear old thing. I don't blame him, not really. These things happen. And I do feel sorry for him, what with the trouble over my disposal and everything.

My *full* name is - was - Charlotte Mary Adams, *neé* Baxter, although no-one called me Charlotte since I was four, except when I'd snapped the end off something.

(mix with)

GRAMS:
Shirō Sagisu – On The Precipice Of Defeat (Loop)

It was always Char. Char, and, later, Auntie Char, and, eventually, *Great* Auntie Char. I lived a full life; and eighty-two isn't such a bad old age, after all. But I was shocked when I realised it didn't end. I suppose everyone is. They don't *tell you*, see – well, they *can't*, really, seeing as how no-one ever comes back, not when they've gone all the way. You see, when you die, there's just a pause.. you feel your body turn off, and then there's nothing for a bit, just... *expectation*, all *clinical*, like when you're sitting in a doctor's waiting room and someone's nicked all the good magazines. And then, you just.... go on. Your mind does. Somehow your consciousness just *keeps going,* like it was separate from your body all along. You don't *feel* anything anymore, of course – which is a godsend to those of us who plumped for cremation, I can tell you. It's quite fun, in fact – you lay there and think, *oh, there go my eyeballs,* and *that's my shin, popping in the flames.* Quite a game, in fact. But you don't *feel* it, because your consciousness is no longer connected to your nerve endings, which are a fizzling liquid on the floor of the furnace with all your other fleshy bits anyway.

Tim's got himself down for organ transplants. He's a bugger for all those '24 Hours in A&E' programmes on telly, so he'll love that, watching them take all his bits and bobs out.

Us cremated folk get the best of all worlds, really. It must be boring as hell for people who are buried – just staying in one place, forever, watching the world go past without you. Could be soothing, I suppose. Although a bugger if they eventually plop a Sainsburys Metro on top of you. But when they burn you, your consciousness stays together as long as your remains do. I suppose some people could get stuck on the mantlepiece for eternity, which would be horrible, watching your other half do all those annoying things without being able to criticise. But me, I've had quite a ride, since I died. Too much of an adventure, really. But you know me. Always time for one last adventure, I always say.

GRAMS:
244sJC – 30 (Edit)

I caused it all, I suppose, with my silly will. I'd always loved the canal that used to run by our school when I was young, and I didn't think there'd be any problem with having my ashes scattered there. I was never a religious woman, not really. Just enough to be polite. *You* know. So as far as I was concerned, once you were gone, you were gone, and nobody much minded what was done to you.

Turns out, though, people *do* mind. The Waterways Authority minded very much that I was going to merge with their precious canal. So much so that they sent a pompous e-mail virtually threatening my poor family with prosecution if they so much as took me *near* the bloody thing. And bless my family, they weren't having any of it. *(sadly)* Not so much Tim, of course. The whole business with running me over brought his thyroid back, and he was in the box room with the curtains drawn, mostly. It was our Kenny, my nephew, always the bright one, always full of sparks. 'If Auntie Char wants to be scattered in the canal, then that's what should happen', he shouted. *(chuckles)* Oooh, he did have a good old go at them. Gorilla warfare, he called it, although I never really got what it had to do with gorillas. 'We'll sneak down in the dead of night, nobody will know. We'll show 'em', he said. 'We'll give Char a proper old send-off'.

They couldn't get anywhere near the school, of course. Shame, that, because the canal was lovely through there. The only bit they could get to without climbing through people's back gardens was beneath the M46 where there's that scabby old path down under the flyover. It was what they call a small gathering, just Kenny and his Polish wife Čensca, their daughter Angelica, who is eight and likes unicorns and *Paw Patrol,* Tim, on his zimmer with a bit of black ribbon tied on, bless him, and Roger, Tim's brother, Kenny's father, who hasn't spoken a word since 1985 when he took against Malcolm McClaren for using 'Madam Butterfly' in a pop song. Pouring with rain, it was, and they had to get a torch to see what they were doing with my box. They put you in a box, you see – at the funeral home. It's a box with a bag in it, and a bag with you in it, and a ribbon round the bag; and the whole thing has a special spring mechanism in it so that when you pull the ribbon the ashes scatter out, cleanly and completely, committing you to the winds or water of whatever place you choose. *Ever* so clever. Saves you scraping around for the remnants of your loved one with a pencil. It's a good idea, really. Under normal circumstances.

F/X: RAIN. CARS DRIVING PAST

(over)

GRAMS:
Plain Characters – Fingerprint City (Loop)

So they took me down to the flyover, under the M46. Used to be just a cart track, when I was a girl, I remember. Dead of night, it was. 'Less people to see and report us to the Waterways', says Kenny. Little Angelica was tired and grizzling, but Čensca had her pretending it was a *Paw Patrol* adventure. Looking for evil geese to arrest, or something, although I don't know that it was appropriate, her scrabbling around in the dirt with all the syringes and condoms and everything. Running around calling, she was, 'evil geese, evil geese', making a hell of a racket. At one point she ran into one of the big concrete caverns made by the legs of the flyover, and then ran back out a couple of minutes later saying there were no evil geese, but there were two men cuddling, and neither of them had any trousers on. Kenny was so angry! 'Spoiling our Char's funeral', 'public indecency', oooh, he banged on and on. Eventually we all went behind the pillar and that was weird because it seemed that Kenny knew them, and there were all sorts of muttered threats and then Čensca, who might have some funny ideas about cabbage but is nobody's fool, started with 'Kenneth, how do you know them? *Why* do you know them, Kenneth? *Why?*' Well *I* had a few ideas – being dead gives you a wonderfully expanded perspective – but, you know, given my situation, I wasn't really in a position to share.

Now, not understanding any of this, young Angelica has taken ownership of my box, and is busily conducting her *Paw Patrol* investigation in a bunch of reeds by the side of the canal. Unluckily for her, this clump of reeds really *does* contain some evil geese, and they are *not* best pleased at Angelica stomping into the middle of them. The geese make a bee-line, or a goose-line, I suppose, for Angelica, who screams, throws my box into the canal and turns to run away, falling face-first into a puddle of mud and green, evil-smelling goose poo. As I float off down the canal, my soul, or whatever it is, watches them recede into the distance, Angelica splashing and screaming, Kenny and two men without pants running around and waving their arms, Čensca crying against a massive concrete pillar.

Well, I think. *This is a turn-up.*

F/X: GENTLE WATER LAPPING SOUNDS

(over)

GRAMS:
Brian Eno – Another Green World (Loop)

It was quite peaceful, floating down the canal. They make your bag and your box nice and sturdy, at the funeral home; watertight, too, thank the lord.

F/X: DUCKS QUACK, CONTENTEDLY

For a while it was just me, and the canal, and some inquisitive ducks, and the distant noise of the motorway. Then I got stuck in a clump of weeds by the bank, hemmed in by a battered coke can, and spinning slowly, like a tired old twin-tub. And there I would have stayed, if it wasn't for spotty boy.

GRAMS:
214sJC – Nelson's Theme (Exilon Dance)

I heard mumbling, first. Then I was poked with a stick, not a very nice feeling, even when you're inanimate. 'What the buggery is this, then', he says, and I'm picked up and peered at by this sallow youth with spots and pinpricks for eyeballs. 'This could be nice', he says, and stashes me into a canvas shoulder bag where I find myself amongst fag ends, bits of foil and half-eaten sandwiches in their packets. Bump, bump,

bump, very uncomfortable it was, notwithstanding not feeling anything. Very disorientating. Until finally I'm out of the bag again and in the messiest, dirtiest room I've ever seen. Tim would have had a heart attack, he's such a stickler for cleanliness, he wouldn't half moan if he found so much as a bit of satsuma peel under the sofa. This place would have given him a bloody coronary. Half-empty food cartons, beer cans, tatty old clothes everywhere, and perched on top of everything there's overflowing ashtrays full of what looked very much like the ends of drug cigarettes. Oh, the *filth*.

And my rescuer is dancing around the room to some... well, I suppose I have to call it 'music', that he's put on. Then another one appears at the door, just as bright as the first, wearing nothing but mouldy old jogging pants covered in stains, scratching his head, asking 'what the bloody f-word is going on.' 'Found some shit by the canal', says my hero, classy as always. 'Fancy box. Could have jewelry in it.'

Oh no, I think. *Not like this. Please.* They both loom over me, and I see the one who plucked me from the water reach down for my ribbon.

F/X: POLICE SIRENS APPROACHING

No sooner does he touch it than the door explodes inwards, and all these policemen rush in, yelling for England.

F/X: POLICE SIRENS, DOOR SHATTERING, SHOUTING

'Nobody move', they're shouting, 'keep your hands where we can see them', just like the games we used to play in the war. The spotty boys are bundled into a police car, and so am I, in a PVC bag, along with other bits and bobs from the table. There's a rolling machine like dad used to have, lots of bits of what look like Play-Doh in freezer bags, and a pipe made out of glass, which is a silly idea, if you ask me, you might chew the end off and get shards.

Finally, we get to the police station, and the spotty boys are up at the desk, being read their rights, just like on *The Bill,* and a very jubilant-looking WPC is making an inventory of all their belongings in a big desk notebook. Everything she picks up, she declares what it is, and writes it down. Very studious, she is, and making a big show of everything. *She's enjoying this,* I think.

And then I think:

I don't like the look of where this is going.

GRAMS:
Jimmy Cauty - Neptune (Edit)

'And what have we got here', she says, with a wry eyebrow, 'pick'n'mix?' Do you know, all my life I'd never been sure how you make an eyebrow go wry. I mean, you always read it in books, but I'd never really seen a wry eyebrow before. Nice to have a new experience, even if it is a bit late in the day.

'Don't know what that is', says spotty boy, sullenly. I'd really taken against him, you know. All attitude and pus. You never used to have his type in the days of National Service. It smartened them up, taught them some respect. If there was a war on, he'd be polishing boots and happy, not sniffing paint and covered in acne. Back in my day, the policewoman would have taken him up an alley and given him a slap. Except she'd be a man, of course.

'Nice box', she says, all sarcastic, like. 'Yours, of *course.* Even though it's not your...style. Bit *flowery,* for you, isn't it, Nelson?'

Forget it, then, I think. *Forget the box. You don't care, I don't care, he doesn't care, let's all go home. Put the kettle on. Let's have a cup of tea, and lets all be friends, and let's never,* ever *care about the stupid old flowery box.*

[silence]

'Shall we look, then?' she says.

GRAMS:
Jimmy Cauty – Saturn (Edit)

The very last thing I remember is fingers tugging impatiently at the ribbon, and then the look of surprise on the young policewoman's face as I accelerated towards her. After that, nothing. After that... just being trapped here, in my last moments, as I fade away altogether. Before that... well, before the nothing there was *something,* and before the something, there was....

....Char.

F/X: DUCKS QUACKING HAPPILY

GRAMS:
Robert Smith – Small Hours (Edit)

END

- 7 -
THE MOVEMENT OF WATER

*Come in, young'uns, gather round.
I'll make sure you're tightly bound.
More evil nights I've never seen
than this accursed Hallowe'en.
Tonight the dead shall walk abroad
and roam the land in evil hordes.
So close the door on wind and hail
and sit ye down to hear my tale.
For you, my chicks, shall have a story:
It's time for Hallowe'en Hellanory.*

Jonathan:

The Movement Of Water began when I was on a short visit to my friends Ian and David who own a canal boat (see *Char*). Ian told me a story about something that had happened on the cut over the summer; a family had been on holiday together, and the mother had fallen off the back of the boat as it was leaving a lock and nobody had noticed until they'd got a long way down the canal, thinking she was safe inside. Her end, as far as I was told the story, was very similar to Maureen's; she as trapped by the huge force of the lock currents and drowned. Whether or not she later came back to haunt and then murder her husband was unreported.

'What a uniquely grotesque way to die', I thought to myself. 'Absolutely perfect for a Hellanory story.'

I'd already been toying with the idea of a Hallowe'en special, as we'd been getting some nice crits on various horror fiction pages, and I wanted to see if I could write a proper, straightforward, suspenseful horror story with all the audience manipulation, the slow building of tension, the false reveals and all that. And then I kind of accidentally committed myself to if in an off-the-cuff comment on the Facebook page, so that clinched it. I was going to kill someone on a narrowboat on Halloween.

In the end, of course, I ended up killing two people. Maureen, like Char, never actually appears in the story as a living person, her death occuring within the first few seconds, but I wanted to keep it very bald and low-key, and set against the soothing, relaxing sounds of the canal. As I started putting it together, after finishing the script, I quickly realised I was taking quite a step away from the usual

Hellanory format, where music drives the narration. This was all about atmosphere, and the sound effects were going to be at least as important as the music. So, rather than music to play her to sleep, poor Maureen just got a 'rounded plop', and the buzzing of flies.

John Vertigan is a man with a stolen name. A bloke I work with, who has, oddly, since become my boss, is called 'Luke Vertigan', and I just think it's an intensely cool name. Not only does it sound kind of futuristic, like a space commander or something, but I suspect that people with this name could be distant descendents of the Vortigan who invited the Anglo-Saxons over here to sort out troublemakers. And who, surely, must therefore have more claim to shaping the history of this island than almost anyone else I can think of.

John Vertigan, on the other hand, is a twat. I tried to make him as unlikeable as possible and give him no redeeming features whatsoever so that both the listening audience and I would be perfectly happy when I finished him off. A deserving death always leaves a sweeter taste.

I should add that my boss is very nice, and not a twat.

If you want an idea of Carole, imagine a slightly more normal Ange from Abigail's Party. That's kind of what she was modelled on, for some reason. Terry is of ample size, and has a beard, largely because most people called Terry should. I like Terry.

SIDENOTES

One of the things I'm most proud of with *The Movement of Water* is the fact that I created my own original sound effect. I was in my local pound shop when I saw a stainless steel moulded ashtray, and I thought 'if I buy that, and take it home, and record myself pinging it with my fingernail, and then slow it right down and put a tiny bit of reverb on it, that might sound like something scary knocking on the hull of a narrowboat.'

And so I did.
And it did.

And at least if we never become famous, I'll always have the ashtray.

F/X: NIGHT SOUNDS, COUNTRYSIDE. OWLS HOOT. GENTLE LAPPING OF WATER. SOMETHING TAKES PONDEROUS STEPS THROUGH THE WATER, THE SOUND GROWING LOUDER AS IT GETS NEARER, INTO:

GRAMS:
Hellanory Theme Tune/Rhyme

F/X: GENTLE LAPPING OF WATER. CANALSIDE BIRD SONG

NARRATOR:
In one way, that is to say from John Vertigan's point of view, Maureen had the most tranquil death imaginable. She made no noise, save for a surprised little squeak as he tipped her off the back of the boat, and the sound of a gentle movement of water, hardly a splash, more like the rounded plop of a stone, as she slipped under the surface. There was no screaming reappearance, no shattering of the surface like glass, no splashing and calling and begging for life; nothing disturbed the gentle, childhood silence of the canal. In the background, like the grains of dried oil paint on a landscape seen up close, the gentle buzz of winged insects around the lock, and a solitary, distant bark of a heron.

F/X: HERON BARKING

In the other way - that is to say from her own viewpoint - Maureen's death was not tranquil at all. She never reappeared from beneath the surface of the canal because the boat from which she fell - with some assistance - was idling in a lock, and the forward paddles had just been opened in order to empty the lock and allow the boat to continue its journey downhill. She had no sooner slipped beneath the matt green surface than she was captured by the immense current of water being sucked down, down into the newly-opened hole in the floor of the lock, through the sluice and into the canal beyond. And, subject to forces of physics way beyond her control, the unfortunate Maureen was sucked down with it, and rammed into the sluice and paddles with such force that she stuck there, like a dog shit that someone had tried to force through a sieve. Her life ebbed away with the silt and the filth of the canal, as the boat - out of the lock now - lubbed and chugged away, leaving behind only stillness, nature's warm summer silence, and little bits of Maureen, suspended in solution.

F/X: WATER RUSHING THROUGH SLUICE

Neither could Maureen expect her sudden disappearance from the canal boat to excite much attention. Of the two couples who had hired it for their 'boozy getaway week', John and Maureen were well known for their constant bickering and violent, drink-fuelled rows, constantly storming off in opposite directions, threatening never to see each other again, only to reappear a few days later as if nothing had happened. They had rowed late into the previous night; neither Carol or Terry would be alarmed, or, frankly, even surprised, to be told that Maureen had stomped off into the nearest village to get a bus to the nearest train station, stopping only to drown her sorrows at the nearest pub with the aid of the nearest bottle, and possibly the nearest single bloke.

The more John examined things in the hazy summer warmth - and the additional hazy warmth of his breakfast brandy - the more he began to see how his momentary impulse at the lock might just turn out to be his release from Maureen forever. In all honesty - and he was an honest bloke, he told himself judiciously - he didn't hate Maureen. He'd never seriously even considered killing her. In a way, he had even loved her, sometimes, with the strange and childlike dependence that comes from a shared alcoholism. There were little bits of Maureen that he'd always really liked – her wicked sense of humour, her motherly concern, her occasional moments of downright filthy sensuality. And, of course, the fact that her giro arrived on alternate weeks to his. But she was too clingy, too demanding. Yes, there were little bits of her he liked, but the whole thing was too much.

If he hadn't have done what he'd done, hadn't raised his toe behind her behind, consigned her to the depths and left her in the sluice, she would have followed him forever. When he was drunk, and free, and didn't have to answer to anybody, she was just too... *there*. Always there. In his face, not giving him room to... stretch. And now, he realised with a sudden burst of endorphins, she wasn't there. She was... somewhere else. And now he really was free, free to be free, free to do what he wanted, and say what he wanted, and go to bed with who he wanted, maybe even mousey Carol, whose demur petiteness had always driven him crazy for some reason. It would be amusing to see if he could pull it off, right under Terry's nose. As it were. The double-entendre made him giggle.

We want to be free! he announced to the gently lopping canal, the drooping willows and sulking herons.
What are you on about? asked Carol, poking her head through the hatch and staring at him.
We want to be free, to do what we want to do, he informed her, seriously. *And we want to get loaded.* He looked back at the shrinking lock, the innocent, green, unbroken stillness, smiled, and murmured to himself. *We want to have a good time.*

GRAMS:
Loaded – Primal Scream (Looped Edit)

What I don't understand, said Terry, languidly, *is why you two don't just sort it out and settle down.* His voice had all the drunken reasonableness of the mild-mannered alcoholic, to whom all problems are eminently solveable if only everyone would keep calm. It was past midnight, and the three of them were lounging on the boat's fold-up sofa seats, empty glasses and bottles covering the table between them. *These... volcanic eruptions of yours are so unnecessary. It's such a waste of effort.*
They're as bad as each other, that's the problem, said Carol. *You* - she jabbed her finger at John – *ARE. AS. BAD. AS. EACH. OTHER.* As she was listing badly to one side, the final finger-jab was misjudged, and landed under John's armpit. John took the opportunity to stiffen his upper arm

muscles in order to give the finger a squeeze, hoping that this might be vaguely sexual, but suspecting that it was just a bit weird.

I can't help thinking... I think she's gone for good this time, he sighed, trying to sound resigned, but sounding more like he'd suffered a mild stroke from the exertions with his bicep.

Bollocks, said Carol and Terry, in perfect unison. While Terry seemed content that he'd covered all the bases perfectly eloquently, Carol decided to unpack her remark a little further. *You always say this. Every time you have a row and one of you storms off, it's always 'the end', you're never going to see her again, and then the following week everything's back to normal. It's just what you two do.* As she spoke, John was slowly shaking his head from side to side, as if the weight of his nose was making it into a pendulum. He wondered if he'd be able to stop.

No. It's different this time. I know. She was totally... different from before. When she left.

Rubbish. Different how?

She seemed... I don't know. She was just different. She was... There was a pause. *...deeper, somehow.* A little noise escaped from his throat, and a tiny bubble of snot expanded at the opening of his left nostril. Shortly afterwards, he went to the boat's small toilet and shower room, where Carol swore she could hear him crying, while Terry, getting more beers from the fridge, said it sounded more like stifled giggling.

F/X: LOUD, METALLIC UNDERWATER CLANG

GRAMS:
Bruton Horror Classics – Cold Sweat (Loop Edit #1)

Whereas the noise that woke him at four in the morning sounded to John like a loud, metallic 'clang', as if something had struck the keel of the boat. He sat bolt upright in bed, unsure of what had woken him, still half in a dream, straining to hear if there was someone moving around, if Carol or Terry had dropped something or slammed a door, but there was nothing. After a few moments he lay back down, and was just starting to sink back into sleep when he heard it again, quieter, this time.

FX: CLANGING, SOFTER, REPEATED. SLOWLY PAN FROM L TO R

And repeated. More like a slow tapping, or knocking on the keel of the boat. For some reason,in his half-awake state, the noise terrified John. He told himself that it was something trapped in the weeds beneath, an old bike, a shopping trolley, stuck fast and knocking against the hull as it was turned by the current, but he knew that it wasn't. For one thing, it was too rhythmic to be natural, like a slow knocking. And for another thing, he realised with growing alarm, it was moving.

It had started by the foot of his fold-up bed, but now it was slowly moving, moving towards the door into the shower room, towards the front of the boat. Fascinated, and, at the same time, inexplicably terrified, John swung his feet out of bed and padded towards the connecting door to the shower room. The knocking was still creeping forwards, slowly – now it was under the sink, now the shower, heading inexorably towards the prow of the boat. John followed, but as he walked past the shower, he froze.

F/X: DISTANT WHISPERING, INDISTINCT

F/X: RUNNING WATER

There was whispering. He could hear whispers, faint stirrings of air containing half-words, suggestions of a voice, of a monologue of sighs with the occasional hint of meaning. The sounds froze John's insides and caused his heart momentarily to slam against the wall of his chest. It was coming from the plugholes.

For a few moments he stared in horror at the small, circular voids in the floor of the shower and the washbasin. The blackness in their centres seemed to pull him in. Every time his panicking brain managed to convince itself that the sounds were natural, he would pick up a word, gone before he could grasp it, like the impression left by the circle of the sun when you close your eyes. He thought he heard his name, but knew that that couldn't be right; and that scared him even more, because it meant that something had snapped inside his head, and he wondered if this was it, if he was insane now, forever. He thought of being on drugs, he thought of social workers, of lying in gutters, of always hearing the whispered voice, saying things to him he could not hear or understand. He tore himself from the plugholes, compelled to continue walking forward, following the knocking,

F/X: CLANGING, REPEATED. SLOWLY PAN FROM L TO R

which was now under the floor of the little galley kitchen, now the lounge, now the single step that led up to the prow. Feeling sick in his stomach, he manouevred himself into the tiny space at the front of the boat,

F/X: ZIPPER IN PLASTIC

and slowly unzipped the plastic windows that kept out the elements. He pushed his head through and looked down.

F/X: GENTLE LAPPING WATER

The canal looked back at him. Its black, mirrored and unbroken surface laughed at him. What the fuck had he expected? Sea monsters? He laughed nervously, trying to ignore that fact that the empty, featureless water which should have reassured him only made him more nervous for some reason.

F/X: ZIPPER IN PLASTIC

GRAMS:
Bruton Horror Classics – Cold Sweat (Loop Edit #2)

He zipped up the window, feeling as he did so the prickling

of hairs on the back of his neck, ancient fear, ancient alarms from a primal, forgotten part of his brain. He'd seen too many horror movies, he thought, that was his problem. He knew how they worked. His fear was of being reassured by the canal, seeing nothing to scare him, only to turn around and come face to face with... something at the other window, the one behind him, the one nearest the bank. Well, screw it. This was real life, not a horror movie, and he was rational enough to understand his fears and where they came from. Screwing up his courage and berating himself for being so suggestible, he turned quickly around to face the other plastic window.

There was nothing there. Just like, he tried to tell himself, he knew there would be. And no sound either, now, he noticed. The knocking had stopped. There was nothing except the darkness, and the gentle movement of water.

F/X: BOATS, MOORED, GENTLY MOVING

John exhaled heavily. Stupid bastard, he thought. Stupid, gullible bastard. Residual guilt. He was torturing himself, was what this was. Well, that had to stop right now. And a good way to start to stop it, he reasoned, was with a drink. He walked back through the lounge and into the galley, reached down a tumbler from the pine shelf and filled it half full with whiskey from the bottle on the fridge. Holding the glass under the tap at the little sink, he filled the other half with water.

F/X: LIQUID FILLING TUMBLER

Except he didn't. He turned the faucet, but no water ran. He tried turning it the other way. Nothing. He stared at the tap, puzzled for a moment into inaction. He was still staring at it when the finger came out.

F/X: MAN SCREAMS, TERRIFIED

GRAMS:
Bruton Horror Classics – Prelude To Murder Sting

Jesus Christ, *what's going on?* shouted Terry as he barrelled into the galley, closely followed by Carol. *John, what the* fuck *is the matter?*

F/X: BOATS, MOORED, GENTLY MOVING (FADE IN)

John offered no answer at first. He was sitting on the floor against the side of the boat, hugging his knees and crying like a slapped child. Occasionally he pointed lamely at the sink, and then exploded into a renewed fit of sobbing. Terry and Carol comforted him the best they could, which was not very well since John lashed out with his arms every time either of them came too close. In time, however, they managed to coax him back to bed, jabbering about fingers, fingers pointing at him, fingers crooked at him, beckoning him, accusing him. They couldn't make head or tail of it, and decided that it was some kind of alcohol-related psychosis which rest would deal with. Carol, who used to be a mother in a previous life, tucked him into his fold-out cot, still blubbering, while Terry flapped around like men do, trying to think of something helpful to say.

Would you like a sandwich, mate? he asked, solicitously. *Nice bit of cheese and tomato?*

He doesn't want a bloody sandwich, Terry, snapped Carol. *He's in shock, not a WI meeting.*

Well I don't bloody know, do I? Terry objected. *Bloody hands coming out of the sink, how the hell am I supposed to know?* He wandered off towards the galley, still muttering to himself. Carol ran a hand across John's forehead – more because she'd seen people do it in films than for any other reason. Then, to complete the mental picture, she held one of Terry's trembling hands between both of her own, and smiled reassuringly at him, the kind of smile a nun would give a sickly child as they waited for the aeroplane to rise up into a sky full of disaster. She was still smiling as Terry reappeared, a whiskey tumbler chinking in one hand and a plate of biscuits in the other.

F/X: ICE CHINKING IN GLASS

Here you go, buddy, he said, cheerfully. *You poured yourself a drink, but you haven't touched it. Seems to be something up with the water, so I've put some ice in it instead. And since you don't want a sandwich -* he glared pointedly at Carol – *I bought you a plate of biscuits. In case you wake up and want a nibble.* So saying, he took one of the small brown sticks from the plate and popped it in his mouth, which made his next words a little indistinct.
Cadbury's Fingers, he explained helpfully, showering them with crumbs.

**GRAMS:
System 7 – Sirenes (Tranquility Mix)**

He didn't know how the hell he managed to get back to sleep, but sleep he must have, because he dreamed, haunted, whispering dreams, the gentle lapping of the water outside accusing him with its hypnotic murmering. *You left me behind,* the water said. *You left me behind, mashed like a potato, torn and bleeding, you left me. I was of the air, and the earth, and you pushed me down, tore me from this world. Of the air and the earth was I, and now I am of the water. I am of the water and I will always follow you, as water always flows downhill.*

He jerked awake, with the words still running through his head like a stream.

**GRAMS:
Bruton Horror Classics - Undying**

I am of the water, he said to himself, and then shook his head, trying to let reality assert itself. Just at that moment, part of his short-term memory helpfully fired up, reminding him of the drink that Terry had left by his bedside, still untouched.

F/X: ICE CHINKING IN GLASS

He groped for it groggily, hearing the remains of the ice-cubes chink against the tumbler, and poured half of the beautiful liquid down his throat in a fiery, glowing path. Jesus, that felt better. The crack under the blinds showed the dawn just beginning to break, little more yet than a suggestion of relative brightness along the line of the horizon. *Might as well get dressed,* John Vertigan thought to himself. *Finish my drink, go out for a bracing walk as the sun comes up. Get some fresh air and clear my bloody head.* He downed another swig from the glass, feeling the ice brush against his lips. He took one of the cubes into his mouth, swilling it around to cool the liquid on his tongue, swallowed, and spat the ice back into the glass. At the same time, he reached with his free hand and turned on the bedside lamp.

The room looked perfectly normal. So normal that he began to realise that he'd dreamt the whole bloody thing. Everything was where he left it, everything was familiar.

F/X: ICE CHINKING IN GLASS

Smiling at his own drunken stupidity, he raised the tumbler in a toast. *To absent friends* he thought, giggling a little as he lifted the last of the whiskey to his lips. And something at the back of his brain saw something in the tumbler, in the same way something at the back of your brain sees that that car ahead of you on the motorway has stopped and you are about to hit it, very fast. The back of John Vertigan's brain saw the two half-melted cubes of ice the glass contained, rolling in the last dregs of golden liquid, and each containing a single, lifeless and incurious eyeball.

F/X: MAN'S TERRIFIED SCREAM

F/X: GLASS SMASHING

John screamed, and flung the glass from him with both hands. It smashed against the wall, and the two eyes landed on the wooden floor with a plop.

F/X: PLOPPING SOUND, EYES MOVING AROUND SQUELCHILY

One of them burst slightly, and a clear juice, flecked with red, began to ooze from it. Because of this, it couldn't swivel quite as successfully as the other, which now seemed to be watching John closely, rotating to follow him as he backed away, through the door into the shower room, screaming as he went.

The windows were shut, and there was no breeze. Despite this, the connecting door closed softly behind him.

F/X: THIN WOODEN CONNECTING DOOR SHUTTING FIRMLY

F/X: MORNING BIRD SONG

I had crazy dreams last night, Terry remarked over coffee the following morning. *Lots of water. Sounds of gushing water everywhere. And screams.* He laughed. *For a while, I thought we'd sprung a leak in the bathroom,* he said. *I dreamed that there was all kinds of hell going on in there. Like going through a lock, it was that loud.*
Now that's strange, Carol said, thoughtfully. *I dreamed about water, too. Really unsettling dreams. Can't remember much about them now, though.* She laughed. *My God, perhaps our dreams are in synch.*
Well at least we didn't have grisly dreams about fingers, Terry replied. *Poor John. He probably took a shower in the middle of the night to clear his head. I wonder if he's slept it off yet?*
We should really wake him up in a moment and see, said Carol. *We need to set off quite early if we're going to reach Ayelsbury by tea-time.*
I'll pour him some coffee, said Terry. *You never know, he might even want that sandwich now.* Carol flicked him the V-sign. Nothing daunted, Terry poured a mug half full of coffee from the percolator, carried it through the shower room, and knocked loudly on John's door.

F/X: KNOCK ON WOODEN DOOR

John, mate. Coffee. When this brought no response, he knocked again, and, after a moment's politeness, quietly let himself in.

F/X: KNOCK ON WOODEN DOOR (SHORTER)

F/X: WOODEN CONNECTING DOOR , OPEN

A few minutes later, he reappeared in the galley.

F/X: WOODEN CONNECTING DOOR, CLOSE

Well, that's strange, he said. *He's not there. He must have got up early and gone for a walk.*
Probably wanted to clear his head, I expect, replied Carol. *He must have the hangover from Hell.*
Not such a bad idea, Terry mused. *It's going to be another beautiful day. Do you fancy a stroll along the towpath before we set off? We'll probably bump into him while we're out there.*
Good idea, said Carol, nodding. *Hang on, I'll just put my contacts in, and we'll go. I can't see a bloody thing otherwise.* She squeezed past him through the tiny doorway into the shower room,

F/X: WOODEN CONNECTING DOOR, CLOSE

and went through the morning ritual of taking her contact lenses from their case, giving them a wash under the taps, which now seemed to be working again, and positioning them carefully onto the surfaces of her eyes, blinking and screwing up her eye sockets in order to get them into place. Her vision was always a bit blurry for the first few minutes when she did this. And that was the reason that as she left the room, she failed to spot something pink on the floor of the shower, something alien, something that very definitely shouldn't have been there.

Had she looked, she would have seen something like a pencil eraser, or perhaps a fancy boiled sweet. But she didn't.

And had she then looked more closely, she would have seen that it was the tip of a man's finger, incongruous and very slightly twitching, slowly sliding down, down, into the plughole. But she didn't do that, either. She just left the room, and climbed, with Terry, through the prow window, zipping it behind them, leaving nothing but the empty narrow boat rocking gently behind her, the watery sun starting to creep across the lounge carpet, and, as if from far away, the gentle, soothing sound of the movement of water.

GRAMS:
Albatross - Fleetwood Mac

The following day, Terry and Carol were sitting at a canalside cafe, just a few hundred yards from the boat, on the edges of town. They hadn't moved on to Ayelsbury, having decided to wait and see if either John or Maureen reappeared, shame-faced and sober, as was often their way.
It's crazy both of them going off like that, said Carol, *without a word or anything. It's almost creepy.*
Creepy? Creepy how? replied Terry, not one to make a crisis out of anything less than global extinction.
Oh, I don't know, i*t's like* Ten Little Indians, said Carol, *like Agatha bloody Christie. Maybe you'll disappear next.*
Terry laughed uproariously. *You're not so lucky*, he said. *I don't intend going anywhere. I'm enjoying my holiday. Besides, it needs two to drive the boat.*
Pilot. She finished her sandwich, pecking at crumbs on her plate like a bird with fingers.
Oh, it's alright, you can still call me Terry.
Carol screwed up her cash-and-carry doily and threw it at him.
The verb is pilot. *You* pilot *a boat. Cretin.* She sighed, absent-mindedly stuffing sachets of sugar and ketchup into her handbag to replenish supplies. *I just wish they'd let us know they're alright. I wonder where they are? I hope they've found each other and made it up. John always said there were bits of Maureen he really loved.*
Yes, Terry countered sagely, pulling at his Drum Gold rollie like a guru, *but that's the thing. You never get to spend your life with just bits of people ...*

F/X: FAINT WHISPER

...Sorry?
Sorry what? said Carol.
I thought you said something.
Not me.
There was a pause, both adrift for a moment in their own thoughts, as if listening to nothing. Eventually, Terry broke the silence, inconsequentially, by saying,
I'll tell you what, though. This tea is bloody good. Really strong. I don't think I've ever had a cup like it.
It is really nice, Carol concurred, looking at the menu in its faux-leather binding. *Ah. And here's why – look.* She pointed at the small print. '*Made with local water*'.
Again the silence returned, shot through with the sound of teenagers riding bikes along the trunk road behind the fields.

F/X: FAINT WHISPER

What? said Carol.
What? said Terry.
Oh, nothing, said Carol, closing her handbag with finality and throwing back the rest of her tea. *I thought I heard you whisper something, that's all.*

GRAMS:
Down By The Water (Edit) - P J Harvey

END

- 8 -
AN OPEN FIRE

'T'is the night before Christmas
so let's take a look in this dusty,
ancient, leatherbound book.
Its festive tales of weirdness and gloom
will keep you enthralled as you meet your doom.
So come in, my dear, and hang up your coat.
Then I'll pour acid right down your throat.
As you gasp and gurgle I'll choose a story.
Have a very Merry Christmas from Hellanory.

Dave:

What better way to celebrate Christmas, I thought to myself, *than by writing a* Hellanory *episode about an elderly, son-fixated witch who loses her temper and decimates her nursing home on Christmas Eve and wipes out all the residents.*

Actually, that's not what I thought. I didn't even think *I know, I'll write a Christmas* Hellanory *episode about a witch*. In fact, I wasn't thinking about witches at all.

Before Jon came up with the outrageously good *The Movement of Water,* we'd discussed the idea of a *Hellanory* Christmas special. I say 'discussed'. Jon sent me a text asking what I thought about doing a Christmas special and I said *yes* and then we didn't really say any more about it. Then, Jon – the cunning swine – surprised everyone – particularly me – by coming up with *The Movement of Water* for Hallowe'en. Normally, we'll send each other the script for an episode and then the recording well in advance of the actual broadcast so that we can give each other our opinions. Not in this case, though. I listened to the Hallowe'en special in much the same way that everyone else does – lights out, headphones on, a large drink in hand and knowing nothing about what was to come.

The Movement of Water is such an absolutely first-class monster of an episode – in more ways than one – that I suspected that getting Jon to collaborate on a Christmas special too would probably be asking a bit too much. So, not wishing to let the Christmas period go unacknowledged, and with the knowledge that Jon would be listening on Christmas Eve like everyone else – lights out, headphones on, a large drink in hand and knowing nothing about what was to come

- I took upon the task of writing an episode for Christmas Eve and *An Open Fire* is the result.

It started life some years ago in the shape of a bit of flash fiction called *Taking Granny For A Spin*, which went like this:

> **Every other Sunday, I take Granny for a drive in the country. It gives her a change of scene from the four walls of her nursing home.**
>
> **I tell her about what I've been doing since I last saw her, although to be honest telling her anything is pointless as she can't even remember who I am.**
>
> **It's quiet around the country lanes, so I push the car to 90mph.**
>
> **'Are you enjoying the drive, Granny?' I ask. But she never replies.**
>
> **Maybe she can't hear me above the roar of the engine. I suppose I really should untie her from the roof rack.**

I tried adapting the above into a full, 15-minute script, turning Granny into Harriet and the driver of the car into Raymond. Harriet became the narrator of the story, chatting away about the people in her nursing home until the very end where, her voice increasingly loud, it's revealed that Raymond's tied her to the roof rack.

It didn't really work.

So I changed it. I turned Raymond into a serial killer, although Harriet was blissfully unaware of the fact. I wanted to have a big reveal at the end, which the listener would get but which Harriet wouldn't, where it was blatantly obvious that Raymond had been despatching his previous girlfriends because Harriet had never approved of them and he had a weird mother fixation. But that didn't work either, and I felt that *My Name Is Michael Crane* had said all I really wanted to say about serial killers. Did I really need to go off down that road again? No, I bloody didn't.

I can't actually remember where the idea of turning Harriet into a witch came from. But when the idea arrived, everything else seemed to fall into place. I like the way

Harriet never actually states *I'm a witch*. There's a casual reference to a cauldron, then other references to casting spells, but that's about it.

Well ... and the fact that just before the opening theme there's a loud thunder clap and an evil witch's cackle. But *apart* from that ...

SIDENOTES

In a break from tradition, I decided to have a sort of pre-credits type scene, rather than start as we had done all through season one with the theme and then the rhyme. I wanted to do it to change things up a bit and because I liked the idea of a thunder clap, then an evil cackle, then the opening theme. A bit like the opening of *The Shakespeare Code* from David Tennant's days in *Doctor Who*. Jesus. Don't get me started on *that*.

Mostly, though, I did it to annoy Jon. You see. I *told* you I'd get him back, the rotter.

Attentive readers will notice the use of *Limu Limu Lima* by The Real Group in this episode. It was also used as the closing music for *Surplus Baggage*. This time round, though, I reversed it, slowed it down and added ludicrous amounts of echo to create an eerie, Christmas background. Or what I think passes as an eerie, Christmas background, anyway.

GRAMS:
Harps and Bells – Lazarus Hyde

F/X: CRACKLING FIRE

HARRIET:
Ooooh, I do love an open fire. Makes it all so ... well, seasonal. Oh, I know there's all the stuff you see in the shops - the decorations, the tinsel, the fake snow, the tree ... But for me, if there's no open fire, then it's not really Christmas. Shame there's no one left to see this one. They've all gone. (SIGH) Ah well. Merry Christmas, wherever you are. Merry Christmas ...

F/X: SILENCE

... and may the flaming gates of hell swing wide and welcome you in.

F/X: THUNDERCLAP AND EVIL WITCH'S CACKLE

GRAMS:
Hellanory Theme Tune/Rhyme

GRAMS:
Limu Limu Lima (Edit) – The Real Group

F/X: CRACKLING FIRE

Marjorie died two nights ago. December the 22nd. Two nights before Christmas. It brought everyone down. Thinking about it now, of course, I suppose it would, wouldn't it? A death spoils the Christmas mood, if truth be told. At the time, though, it seemed like a ... well, like a *kindness*, really, what with her just ... hanging on to life like that. And not really much of a life. I mean, how much joy can you wring out of a day when you spend most of it just staring at a wall and breaking wind? It was a relief, really. For her *and* me. God, but she were miserable. Oh! Doom and gloom and more doom and some extra gloom thrown in for good measure. With even more doom. Having a chat with Marjorie was like ... like having your soul sucked out through your nose. I've never had my soul sucked out of my nose so I suppose I wouldn't really know, but oh *God*, Marjorie liked a chat. Relentless, she was. I'd see her in the communal living room first thing in the morning before breakfast and I'd forget myself and say *How are you, Marjorie?* - just out of politeness, really – and she'd be off: *Not too good, Harriet*, she'd say. *My back's playing up, my joints hurt, my bowels are none too reliable and ... well, my hips are never going to get any better, are they? Not at my time of life.*

Left you feeling like life wasn't worth living. Honestly. I'd finally tear myself away from her after twenty minutes – twenty minutes? It felt like twenty years – and I'd want to stick my face in a meat grinder I were that desperate. And I kept telling myself, *don't rise to it, Harriet, don't rise to it*. And I didn't. Not for months. I managed to hold myself back until ... until two nights ago ... until Raymond ... and then I ... well. Anyway. In the end ... like I say. It was a kindness. In a way.
(SIGHS)
Poor Marjorie. It was a hell of a fall.

F/X: SCREAM AND HIT

All the way down those stairs and then bang. Head open on the corner of the skirting board. Really quite nasty. She didn't stand a hope in hell of surviving that. Quite proud of myself really. Just goes to show, it's like riding a bike. You might get a bit wobbly in your old age, a bit out of practice, but you never forget how.

I suppose, thinking about it, in a way, she died happy. She banged on about illness and disease and medication and dying that much, you'd have thought death was her life's ambition, so at least she's fulfilled that. I just ... I just wish I hadn't lost me temper, lost me control. Bloody Raymond.

GRAMS:
Tales Of The Unexpected (Edit) – Ron Grainer

F/X: CRACKLING FIRE

It were Raymond's idea, the nursing home. *Why don't you think about going into a home, mum?* he said. I mean, it had been in the back of my mind for a while, if I'm honest. What with Frank gone this last ten years and me living by myself, and Raymond living an hour away and me being a bit unsteady on the old legs ... Well, it was ... oh, what's that phrase people use these days? It was a *no brainer*.

I suppose it wasn't too bad, as nursing homes go. Deathly boring. Nothing ever happened and the food was nothing to write home about. But I had my own little room and I got treated really well so I know I shouldn't really complain. It didn't take me long to make me feel like I belonged and everyone was so welcoming. Arthur dribbling into his scrambled eggs in the morning, Penelope breaking wind every five minutes, and Catherine, dear, dear Catherine and her incessant chatter about her long-dead mother. And that was just the people who worked there. They tried really hard though, what with it being Christmas. The decorations. The tinsel everywhere. The tree in the corner, where Peggy normally sat. She got so annoyed when they told her she had to move. Said she was going on hunger strike and wouldn't eat her Christmas dinner unless they moved the tree. But they didn't move it and she didn't say nowt more about it. Which was a shame. Her going on hunger strike on Christmas Day would have livened things up a bit. *Would* have done. If Raymond hadn't ... Oh ... Poor Raymond. I can't really blame him for what happened. He's never really had anyone else. I mean, there's me, obviously, but ... well. A grown man needs another woman in his life. Not just his mother. It's not healthy. There again, the key thing is to find the right one. It's no good settling for second best. And really, the girls and women Raymond's had, they've just never been ... well, right, in my opinion. And it hasn't been through want of trying on his part. You've got to hand it to him. He's a tryer, is Raymond. But he never got it right. Never got them right. I mean, you could argue, I suppose, that he was lucky if anyone took an interest in him. I mean, as a woman, would I have wanted to marry Raymond? Would I have wanted him next to me in bed at night? Would you? Imagine it. Uuuugh! There you are, full of red wine – well, you'd have to be, wouldn't you, with the prospect of Raymond between your legs and breathing all over you – anyway, there you are, like I say, full of red wine – it'd have to be something strong like that, maybe even stronger, although I've never been able to stomach spirits, even when I was younger – and you're in the throes of red-hot passion – hard to imagine with Raymond involved, I know, but anyway - and you've got him there, banging away and banging on about the price of washing powder or buy-one-get one-half-price packs of chicken breast.

F/X: CUT TO SILENCE

Well. It's hardly *Lady Chatterley's Lover*, is it?

GRAMS:
Crafty Party (Edit) – Gert Wilden

Poor Raymond. He was a late bloomer, he was. That's if he ever really bloomed at all. Never showed any interest in girls until he was about to leave school, after his A levels. Frank wondered if he might be a bit … well, you know … that way inclined. But a mother knows her son better than anybody and … and I would have known. If he was … you know … that way inclined.

The first girl I can remember him bringing home … I can remember what she looked like like it were yesterday … *well*. I ask you. Stripy tights. Black jumper with holes in it. Hair every which way. *Very trendy*, Raymond told me afterwards. *Very punk rock*. Well, I don't know about that, I told him. Looked more like something the cat had dragged in sideways and inside out. *Oh mum*, he goes, *Don't be like that*. So I said to him, I said to him straight, I said, *Raymond, if you think you're bringing* that *back into my house and under my roof again, you've got another think coming. She'll have to go. It's as simple as that. She'll just have to go.* And ... she *went*. I mean, I could see he liked her and all that but she wasn't right for my Raymond. I could see that straight away even if he couldn't and it was my duty, as his mother, to look after him. So I just ... well, gave her a little helping hand. I got my pot down – whatever you might see in films or read in books, it's not a cauldron, more like a saucepan than anything else, and you don't put it over a fire you just stick it over the hob. Then I stirred in the herbs – none of this 'eye of newt and toe of frog' rubbish – and whispered the spell.

F/X: WHISPERING (INDISTINCT)

A week later I said to Raymond, I said to him, *So? Are you seeing her again?* And he said, *No mum. She's gone. She's left town and she's not coming back.* And she never did, as far as I know. Ooooh, he were that miserable I felt ... well, *guilty*, I suppose. But I said to him, I said, *There're plenty more fish to fry, Raymond, I said. Plenty more. A mother knows best. You just need to find the right one.*

F/X: CUT TO SILENCE

But he never did.

GRAMS:
Reversed – Lazarus Hyde

Oh they came at a steady stream. You've got to hand it to Raymond, he certainly didn't give up. They came in all shapes and sizes. And he introduced me to every single one. I can remember them all. And not one of them, not one of them, was right for my Raymond. He couldn't see it. But I could. Well ... a mother sees everything. I were right busy with my pot.

F/X: WHISPERING (INDISTINCT)

I had it set up over a bunsen burner in the shed at the bottom of the garden cause Frank didn't approve of my little ways and carrying on inside the house. I had to vary the spell after the first couple of goes, though, because even Raymond – who's a few peas short of a casserole at the best of times – well, even he started to question why his new girlfriends all seemed to suddenly get the urge to move away after meeting him. I didn't want him getting paranoid. So their fathers started winning the pools or landing sensational jobs in America or Australia. Then I varied it a bit more and gave him terminal B.O. Or paint-stripping halitosis or sweaty feet that could kill a horse at 12 feet. On one occasion – Susan her name was. Oh, but she was a real horror. There was no way she was going to get her hands on any part of my Raymond – on that occasion I gave him B.O., halitosis and sweaty feet all at the same time. He didn't see her for dust. *Good riddance to bad rubbish*, that's what I said.

But of course, the time came when he moved out and moved away, as all children must. I couldn't keep my eye on him all the time, couldn't keep an eye on who he was keeping company with. So I cast a general spell, one that would allow him to ... well, sow his oats, so to speak, because he is a man after all and they do have their needs - but wouldn't allow him to get himself into any sort of permanent arrangement. And over time he sort of accepted his lot in life as a confirmed batchelor. In the end, I didn't even need me pot, didn't need to renew the spell. He'd convinced himself he'd never meet anyone and I retired from me covenly duties.

F/X: CUT TO SILENCE

And then I went to the nursing home.

GRAMS:
Backwards – Lazarus Hyde

Like I said, it were alright. I passed my days in peace, quiet and boredom. I took me pot and me special herbs with me, just in case. Young Debbie, one of the carers, said *Oh you won't need a silly old saucepan here, Harriet* but I gave her one of my looks – one of the looks that lets them get a tiny inkling of what I'm really like inside, full of horror and misery and fire and nightmares – and she never said that again. And I were happy, really. Raymond would come and visit me every two weeks and take me out for a drive in the country. It were the closest thing I ever got to excitement. And he never said owt about lady friends and in the end I stopped asking.

Then, the last but one time he came, just as he was leaving, he said *Mum, next time I come, I'm going to have a bit of a surprise for you*, and he went away grinning like a bloody lunatic. So I'm wondering what he's talking about for two solid weeks. Then he turns up, on Sunday. Two days ago.

F/X: SILENCE

And he's not alone.

GRAMS:
Hungarian Dance No 5 (Edit)

He's only got a ... a *woman* with him. And ... and he's grinning from ear to ear like a Cheshire cat. This is Kathy, mum, he says. And they look at each other, all soppy like, and she puts her arm through his and then he turns and looks at me and says, *Mum, we're engaged. Kathy's going to be my wife.*

Well. I hardly heard the rest of it. I just nodded and smiled as the two of them blabbed on. They'd known each other six months. *Six months.* And in all that time, Raymond had said nowt to me. His own mother. I were in shock. There's this ... this *woman*, this Kathy ... there, sitting *there*, in *my* room, next to my one and only child, *my* son, and holding on to him like she ... like she *owns* him. And she's completely won him over, you can see that. He's all lovey-dovey and fetching her things and laughing at her jokes. And I can feel him ... slipping away. Out of my hands, out of my life. At one point, he says *I'm just off to the loo. Give you two a chance to have a chat.*

And off he goes. And she turns to me and I give her one of me looks and … and she doesn't even flinch. She just looks me back, right in the eye, and I see it in her. Horror and misery and fire and nightmares. And she smiles at me. And she says, *Don't worry, Harriet.*

F/X: SILENCE

I'm *looking after him now.*

**GRAMS:
Horror Choir – Lazarus Hyde**

After they'd gone, and I was left brooding, turning things over in my mind, I knew I weren't needed no more. On the one hand, I knew that Raymond would always be looked after, if not by me then by one of my … well, one of my kind. Which I suppose is a blessing. On the other hand … I'm redundant. Left hanging out to dry like old knickers. And although I know that's the way it has to happen, that's the order of things, … *I'm not happy about it.*

I have to say, I were proper miffed. I didn't go down for dinner that night. Said I weren't feeling a hundred percent. And I'm up in my room and I can hear Marjorie downstairs, banging on as usual about her hips, her eyes, her bowels … oooh, nothing was right. So I said to myself, I said *You know what, Marjorie?* Why don't we just put you out of your bloody misery, once and for all. I didn't know what I was doing. I was in such a rage. I dug out me pot and me bunsen burner from under the bed, I mixed some herbs and I said the spell and later that night …

F/X: SCREAM AND HIT

Marjorie came a cropper on the stairs.

And it would have been fine … I suppose … if I'd stopped there. But … I didn't. I *couldn't*. I couldn't get Raymond and that … that Kathy out of my head. Seeing them walk off and out through the door, arm in arm, not looking back – he always used to look back, always give me a little wave, but not this time, didn't give a toss about me – and remembering that look she'd given me. Well ... something ... something snapped in me head. That was my Christmas ruined. And I thought ... and it were selfish, I know ... but I thought if *my* Christmas is ruined, then I'm going to ruin everyone else's.

F/X: WHISPERING. DEMONIC SOUNDS RISING TO A SCREAMING CRESCENDO

And so tonight, Christmas Eve, I mixed the herbs in me pot – the whole lot, this time – and I said the spell and I said the words that should never be said, but I said them anyway. And then ...

F/X: HUGE EXPLOSION (FADE OUT)

F/X: (FADE IN) ECHOEY ATMOS

Ooooh, I do love an open fire. Makes it all so ... well, Christmassy. Oh, I know there's all the stuff you see in the shops - the decorations, the tinsel, the fake snow, the tree ... But I love a big, open fire. Shame no one's left to see this one. They've all gone. (SIGH) Ah well. Merry Christmas, wherever you are. Merry Christmas ...

GRAMS:
Jingle Bells (Edit)

END

HELLANORY: GENESIS

with apologies to Gene Roddenbery

Contemporary historians often argue over the real starting point of the *Hellanory* story. Some of the more radical and provocative even declare 1965 to be the true beginning, the year that Dave Hopkins was forged in the white heat of technology along with Teasmaids and the Post Office Tower. But the real genesis of *Hellanory* was the summoning, by Dave, of the Alabaster Lumpfish, primaeval demon from the nether dimensions. In taking the bat's wing owned by Young Ralph, the office boy, and reciting the incantation of summons, Hopkins not only succeeded in creating the peerless writing partnership that was to prove so successful, but also set in train a series of events which turned the *Hellanory* staff from an office full of freaks, mutants and misfits into highly successful purveyors of short audio stories. This cataclysmic event is recorded in Young Ralph's diary, and is here transcribed for posterity. There may be some confusion engendered by the fact that so many of the *Hellanory* staff are called 'Ralph'; but you, sweet purchasers of this script book, will most certainly all be familiar with the various protagonists from their pictures on the *Hellanory* Facebook page.

Few will ever know the true story behind *Hellanory*; only you happy few who have stayed with us on the journey so far. Here, then, are the relevant parts of the diary. Dialogue is given in script form; but I have included some of Young Ralph's observational notes in italics to help with the background.

Jonathan Smith

DAVE:
Hail, hail, fire and snow
Naughty Lumpfish, we will go
To the realms of Hellanory
Give us power to tell our stories.

Hail, hail, fire and ice
Twisty Lumpfish, please be nice
Spread our fame o'er land and sea,
Naughty Lumpfish, come to me!

RALPH'S NOTES: *There's a really long pause here. Nobody speaks. Everything is quiet. Plus, we can't see anything because Mr. Hopkins has turned all the lights off.*

DAVE:
Hello?

ALABASTER LUMPFISH:
Hello, dear.

DAVE:
Lights! For God's sake, somebody turn on the lights!

Ralphetta turns on the lights. An old woman is sitting in a rocking chair, knitting what looks like a toilet roll cosy.

DAVE:
Um.

ALABASTER LUMPFISH:
Hello, dear. Sorry, I was waiting for you to finish. It sounded lovely.

DAVE:
Um.

ALABASTER LUMPFISH:
Yes, dear?

DAVE:
Um. I'm afraid there's been a case of mistaken identity, madam. I was looking for a primeval demon.

ALABASTER LUMPFISH:
Yes, dear, I know. That's me. Alabaster Lumpfish, primeval demon of the netherworld, spirit of rheumatism.

DAVE:
Really? I thought you'd – sorry. Spirit of what?

ALABASTER LUMPFISH:
Rheumatism, dear. Spirit of rheumatism. We all have to be spirit of something, you see. Spirit of death, spirit of war, spirit of anguish. Spirit of dark and lonely water, he was on the telly. There wasn't much left by the time I got there, so I had to make do with rheumatism.

DAVE:
Ah.

There's quite a long pause here, during which everyone looks at each other, and occasionally at the Alabaster Lumpfish, who is smiling serenely and knitting away. Eventually, it is Mr. Hopkins who breaks the silence.

Er. Would you like a cup of tea... madam?

ALABASTER LUMPFISH:
Ooooh, that would be lovely, dear. Nice and strong. Two sweetners, if you do them.

Mr Hopkins motions for all of us to follow him into the kitchen. It's a poky little place we have, little more than a cupboard with a Baby Belling and a sink, lit by one dim overhead lightbulb which swings to and fro. The silence as Mr Hopkins puts the kettle on is punctuated only by a single dripping tap. Eventually, Mr Hopkins speaks.

DAVE:
We appear to have summoned an old woman.

RALPH:
Be ye careful, young maister. Oft comes evil in lowly guise.

DAVE:
Yes, I suppose so. But I really wish you'd talk normally, Ralph. We've had this out before. I mean, 'evil often comes in lowly guise' would be much more contemporary. Or even 'watch it, she might be a bit handy.'

RALPH:
As ye say, young maister.

DAVE:
Right, then. And it's 'master', not 'maister'. I don't know that anybody ever said 'maister'. And don't wobble your head at me like that.

RALPH:
Yes, maister.

DAVE:
Okay, then. Ralph?

RALPH:
Yes, Mr. Hopkins.

DAVE:
Do we still have The Partner?

RALPH:
Yes, Mr Hopkins.

DAVE:
Where is it?

RALPH:
In my chest freezer, Mr Hopkins.

DAVE:
Right. Go and drag it out. Let's see what this little old lady can do.

By now, everyone is excited. Ralph disappears into the cupboard under the sink that he shares with Ralphetta, soon to reappear dragging a full-sized man's inert body, covered in scars and amateur stitching, behind him. Ralphetta is rocking and singing her special song to herself, the one about eyes. Ralph is running around the kitchen barking, his head wobbling like a water balloon, while Ralph is sticking his long, hairy tongue into the power points and making his hair stand on end. When everyone has calmed down a little, we all troop back into the office, with me carrying a tray on which stands a doily, and on the doily, a bone china cup with frilly edges and roses, both of which were borrowed from Ralph and Ralphetta's quarters under the sink. The old lady is sitting in the chair as before, completely ignoring Mr and Mrs Ralphington, the cleaners, who have appeared from nowhere and are standing, one on either side of her, staring at her.

DAVE:
Your tea, Madam Lumpfish.

ALABASTER LUMPFISH:
Lovely, dear. Ta.

She sips her tea, while we all look on expectantly, waiting for something to happen.

Ooooh, that's lovely. Really hits the spot, that does. What a pretty cup, too. I must say, dear, you've really got off on the right foot. Does an old demon's heart good, it does. Of course, strictly speaking -

At this moment, every one of us is suddenly wracked by the ache of slowly-chewing ants crawling within the marrow of each and every one of our bones. The light through the office windows is extinguished, and the place is lit cruelly as if by the flames of burning, melting cadavers. The old woman is gone, and in her place is a figure which mocks that of humanity, a beast-like form comprised of screaming, tortured faces and festering stumps protruding from every joint, angle and orifice. Its head is a giant, burning lantern, its voice a voice formed from the hopeless wails of the thrice-dead, twisted and mocking, the sound of souls burning in eternal hell.

I am not old, having neither age nor wordly form. I was, before the dawn of that which you call 'time', I am, and shall be, when time itself is at an end. The passing of aeons does not touch me, nay, nor the endless spinning of the stars.

When we all stopped screaming from the pain, we noticed that the light was back to normal, and, between our sobs, we turned to face what was, once more, a smiling old woman in a chair.

Still a nice cup of tea, though.

She puts the cup down and puts the knitting away into a little bag by her side.

Now. I dare say you'll be looking for some kind of credentials? People generally do.

DAVE:
Well, that was...

ALABASTER LUMPFISH:
Oh, don't mind that, dear. Just me and my silly ways. No, I insist. We have to follow the form. It's traditional for me to do a little something for you to demonstrate my power and dominion, blah blah blah, then you give me your soul and the souls of all your offspring for eternity, and then we get down to the big stuff. Now. What would you like? An enemy crushed? A kingdom overthrown? Someone raised from the clutches of death?

She said this in the voice of someone offering around a plate of biscuits. Which caught us all a bit off-guard, I think.

DAVE:
Ah, please. Well, sort of.

ALABASTER LUMPFISH:
Sort of?

DAVE:
Well, um, I... I made a partner.

At this point, Mr Hopkins seems to feel that he's somehow lost the initiative. Either that, or he feels that the situation isn't as formal as it ought to be, or (more likely) that he isn't showing quite enough respect following the lantern-head incident. He kind of sticks his chest out and stands almost to attention, and says

A partner have I created, oh Lumpfish; from cadavers and fish and bits of stuff I found under motorway bridges. I intended that he should assist me in my writing; dealing with drugs and anal sex and other tawdry matters of which I have no wit, yet which amuse the great unwashed. And yet the spark of life is not within him, despite my best effort. He lies, inert as a... a... um, beanbag.

Ralph's balloon-like head is wobbling with approval during this speech, while the old lady peers at Mr Hopkins over her glasses, unimpressed.

ALABASTER LUMPFISH:
And just what were your best efforts, hmm? Plugging him into the mains? This isn't *Carry On Screaming*, dear. Or did you bung him on the roof and wait for a thunderstorm? Have you ever noticed how that's a guaranteed way to get a ten-week heatwave? Sod's law, that is.

She sighs.

Well, wheel it in, then.

Ralph and Ralphetta drag The Partner in from the kitchen and deposit it at the old lady's feet. She peers curiously at it over her glasses and then jabs one of her knitting needles into each of its nostrils, and screams:

By the Sash of Rassillon!

DAVE:
The Sash of Rassillon? Really?

ALABASTER LUMPFISH:
Don't be silly, dear, I picked your brains. I don't have to shout anything, but it helps with the effect. Makes people feel they're getting their money's worth.

JON:
Jesus Christ.

RALPHETTA:
It lives!

JON:
I'm sorry... 'it'?

And Ralphetta was right. The Partner was sitting up, removing knitting needles from his nostrils and looking around, somewhat perplexed.

DAVE:
My God. It really lives!

JON:
Look, I'm really sorry. 'It'??

ALABASTER LUMPFISH:
Yes, dear, it lives. And it will assist you in your quest for dominion. And it will be called John Smith, for I am a bit bored and I can't be bothered to think of anything more interesting. I tell you what, take out the 'H'. Call it Jon Smith, that's a little bit different. And here -

and at the word 'here', she held out her hand, and the room went dark, becoming lit as if by a pale and sallow light which seemed to emanate from nowhere. She reached out to The Partner, and tore something from his mouth: and suddenly the room was filled with a hellish sound, and infernal 'hhhhhhhhh' noise, like the very breath of Hell -

...take this 'H', which I have ripped from his essence, and send it out into the world: let it be a beacon, an alarm, a warning. We are coming. We are coming, and you will serve us. I will give you dominion, but you will pay me with your soul, and with your stories. One story shall you give me, each fortnight; every fourteenth day, one story you shall bring to me, and they better be bloody good, too.

Slowly, the hellish breathing sound faded, and we all stood dumbstruck at the demon from the darkest depths that sat so innocently before us. She held before her Ralphetta's cup, and, quietly, like a whisper from a coffin, she spoke once more:

Any chance of a refill, dear?

END

www.hellanory.com

Hellanory … Hellanory …
… Season Two Coming Soon …
… Hellanory … Hellanory

Printed in Great Britain
by Amazon